I0551684

THE LONG JOURNEY HOME

The Lanterncup Series

Author: Marcus Tay (12 years old)

Printed in the

United States of America

@2016 Tay's Imagination World.

All rights reserved

ISBN #: 978-0-9964830-4-9

Shadow Clan Territory

Forest of Zoro Rampikes • Payaya
Dock
Arctic Reef
Cold Dunes • Faya
• Kakatab

Tropical Fruit Plantation

outstretched land

Adoiko ~ The Northern Hemisphere

Farmland • Toas
• Tache
Mt. ORSO
Kihusea

Lari
• Toash
CuaC

Goliather's Lair

Motique
Dor

Jungle of Mazes

Gulf of Massive Ice Craters
North Pole

Wall Line
Moof
Tatso
Saik

Underwater Volcanoes

Desert of Longing

Cove

• Yart
Topwa
• Mooka
Forest of Traps

Yun
I.I.I.C.

Island of Perfection
eeeto

Sand Bay

Land of Secrets

Plane Wreckage

The Mountain of Day and Night
= FFFFF = Bistro

Known

Tad

Roost • • Keel

Equator Line

Tevo
Sreki
Crent
Look Right Nill hills
Lotan

Crofan

Teet

Rolathain
Wasteland of Hardships
Forbidden Landscape
Zark

Contents:

Prologue: One-in-Charge

"That was a failed accomplishment!" His Majesty roared exaggeratingly. "I believe what you said was very contradicting." "No…why on earth did you convince me to carry-out such a degrading idea?" His Majesty was extraordinarily furious.

"Hear me out…I-I can explain!" the Colonel nearly screamed at the change of tone from the one he served.

"It was all a way to test our opponents, all right?" the Colonel said, attempting to soothe His Majesty's feelings.

"You deceiver! You guaranteed that it would work as I wished! What other lies have you yet to tell?" His Majesty yelled in the Colonel's face. "Blow it all out!"

The Colonel looked like he was on the verge of sobbing…but didn't probably because it would be embarrassing even in front of one person he knew for a long time.

After all, he did have more muscles than His Majesty.

There was a difference, he knew it from the start to whenever.

1

But the Colonel didn't understand it. He indeed was searching for the correct answer, not a guess.

"We need to move-around ourselves, I cannot accept the fact of losing like this. The world is destined to be in my hands!" His Majesty was saying.

"We have to use our own forces now, it's not going to work if we rely and depend on others. We have to show the world that help is not needed. Besides, are we harming the world? No! We're just going to re-shape the rules. Humans will be in the minority...that's it!! They will be perfectly okay with the change," His Majesty concluded. "What do you think?"

"Oh, really, huh?" the Colonel looked up from the floor. "Yeah, so...?" His Majesty asked back. "That will not be!" "What do you mean?" "I've helped and supported you long enough!" "Not in my standard," His Majesty shot back, his eyes deadly.

"What is it you want to say?" His Majesty questioned alarmingly. The Colonel stood up in a man-like fashion. The leather chair he'd been sitting on squeaked and relaxed, like it broke free of its burden. The Colonel unshaved his curved-sword (the ones pirates used).

2

He swiped it across His Majesty's chest.

His Majesty left his seat and fell face-forth onto the floor.

The Colonel kicked his side around so he was facing him.

His Majesty made an evil grin and breathed a final breath.

His eyes rolled back.

Four words left the Colonel's lips before time even continued.

"REST IN PEACE FOREVER," were the words

PART ONE:
THE SHADOW CLAN TERRITORY

Chapter One: A Perilous Swim

"Life is like a bubble," Alexis Vos spoke softly. She sighed immediately.

Ian rested his head on one hand.

He didn't dare look over the churning waters. It was foggy, but the blue lights still shone. Ian didn't want to think of anything happy, somehow. Was he really becoming more and more miserable? Could his judgement be credible?

Ian thought of his mom. She had made them go on this journey.

Why hadn't she tagged-along? Her name was Lorry.

Pressure was common.

When time is limited, the higher intensity there is of it anywhere and anytime.

Dawn had arrived.

It was far too late to escape trouble.

Maybe Flix, who was a metallic-monkey looking creature (a friend) would figure something out before they reached the territory.

Ian confirmed that Shadow Clan wouldn't be too excited to see them.

Would he be able to explain for at least several minutes?

Adolko was a world of many different terrains. Ian wished there was no such thing as time, and yet everybody would keep on living joyfully.

Ian abhorred being nervous and anxious. Anxiety was always the attribute he wanted to avoid.

Ian couldn't get over the debate in his mind on whether suffering or simply not having a soul was the better case.

Was Shadow Clan really going to give them a chance to express themselves? They were foreign strangers. Wouldn't getting rid of them be better than to put them in prison?

Ian tried thinking from their perspective. How did Shadow Clan consider a problem or threat, they might call the matter? How was the culture?

Ian could die any second. He has never experienced death, but getting to know how it feels is a whole different story.

And yet, entering a new environment was difficult.

Adjusting was the second thing Ian wanted to avoid.

Suddenly the boat rocked violently, they were still in mid-sea.

"What's wrong?" Drake blurted.

"There aren't even any rocks!" Reeve cried worriedly. "This is strange," Jarret added. "Oh no..." Joe said.

Something was happening for sure. "Why?" Ian shouldn't have asked.

Ian didn't like the feeling he suddenly had. Electricity sparkled here and there. It was unpredictable.

Am I going to get stroked-down? Ian inquired from his mind.

His first guess was The Shocker. He definitely was an option. But then his brain lingered to Shadow Clan.

Was this the weather inside its territory? Ian thought of the neon-blue that shone on their bodies.

"Guys...overboard!" Joe launched from his mouth.

Batelo the Moygeri flung herself into the dark-blue waters.

It was murky.

She didn't even wait for her friend Blake.

There was no time to get informed.

Ian dived into the churning waters.

It was freezing cold.

Ian thought of the Titanic.

Was he really going to die like this?

His weight carried him to the bottom.

Ian was always afraid of depth.

Anything could be lurking here, he thought.

Ian appeared.

He gasped for oxygen...*huh, huh, huh.* Ian had to save himself before anybody else. He couldn't hear anything.

Ian rubbed his eyes. Just then, there was a flash of white. Ian slammed into the waters, head-backwards.

He sank 10 feet deep.

A ruffle of bubbles exploded out of nowhere at the surface.

Ian kept his eyes open only for a semi-second.

Floom! Sound was muffled.

It could have come from anything.

Suddenly, the water pressure went higher, and then warm air arrived. Ian took in all the O2 he could in one sputter.

He coughed a few times.

Ian felt rubber.

He was on a beltway where products were shipped on.

It was bumpy.

Ian saw that he was in an oval-shaped tunnel of some sort.

An electronic voice spoke: You are about to be inspected, unknown object.

"What?!" Ian bounced up in surprise. First of all, why did it tell him what was about to start? Ian didn't get the situation he was unfortunately in. Circumstances was a variety of many plots that were possible.

Second of all, why was he called a so-named 'unknown object?' I should have sabotaged the entire mission! Ian thought quickly.

9

Humans were in fact physically weak.

Ian decided to just roll-off the moving rubber-top.

He sat there for like a while…which was an estimated long time.

Ian wanted to stay there…but he knew the job needed to be completed.

Ian stood up and staggered towards where he thought there was light.

Pitch-black darkness was never the best to dwell in.

What if Shadow Clan was here? Confidence was the key, Ian thought.

Ian felt for the low ceiling after standing up. He traced-out a rectangle that was cut and edged into the Styrofoam-protected top.

Ian didn't know what it was, but could he at least try something with the unknown part? Was it worth it? This was a question Ian has faced many times before during his entire life.

He got onto his tippy-toes and jumped-up with his arms extended above his head. It was a hatch to the bottom of the bay.

It flung open. Ian's sense of sight had to be adjusted.

It was wide open, and yet, water didn't rush in at all for a tedious couple seconds. What kind of magic is this? Ian thought.

He was starting to get very annoyed by the point of everything in the territory even though it was still the beginning.

"Shadow Clan is controlling the flow of water and how it moves," out came a voice…a rather familiar one. Flix's!

Ian didn't remember hugging the bulky box of connected metal…who was indeed Flix. It was him at last.

He'd come back! Flix was right…before long, he would show up again.

Flix was my savior! Ian thought.

Or maybe the whole reunion wasn't real.

Ian's head nodded automatically as he awoke in the same pitch-black scenery he was in. Oh, why? He thought.

His eyes were on the verge of shutting again.

Ian focused his attention up.

The dark-slimy water grizzled by. Each current was so thick that it would resemble a line from airplane height, no kidding.

Ian abhorred not being in his comfort zone. Things wouldn't work with him just passing time where he was, Ian figured.

Scenarios weren't always the same, he'd learned from his experiences.

So, the only option was leaving the place he was in. Ian figured finding out what the area was for was important. 'I will come back' he mouthed the words at the ground. And with that, he dove straight-up into the sea.

Ian was trembling with coldness.

Freezing was another issue.

He was literally opening his mouth and screaming while gulping-up large amounts of water at the same time.

It wasn't a good feeling. Ian was about to give everything up.

Sinking seemed like a very tempting option.

No.

Bolts of electricity shot out of nowhere even in the water.

Ian scrambled and swam like a puppy.

He did a swimming-style called the dolphin to avoid areas he thought would be hit with electricity.

News Flash: being a coward was extremely easy…but not in deep sea.

He considered going back to where he came from, which was the place with the moving beltway.

But that place was creepy anyway. Ian tried swimming back several times…but the currents kept pushing him forward.

Ian started panicking. He even punched himself a few times, his feet and legs kicking randomly in the water.

Ian was gaining altitude from the surface. It wasn't good.

Then he found himself levitating…could it possibly be true?

Chapter Two: The Shadivil War

This time it was tangible Flix. Ian was on solid ground again…or not. It was all flat land covered with miles and miles of blackish-brown soil that was somehow wet. 'Ill' Ian's impression was about the place surrounding him.

This was not what he expected. In the distant, there were colors flying into the air. What was all that?

There was blue obviously, and yellow. Was there some kind of celebration? But then he looked at the creature in front of him.

"There's a civil war going on. Both sides are trying to win! I've a lot to tell you…but I beg you, not now.

What you say here is restricted, okay? That's the rule and law!" Flix said rapidly and he started running towards all the commotion. Ian followed, of course.

✳ ✳ ✳

They were about 100 feet from all the turmoil before Flix whispered, "Over here, come." Ian reluctantly went to him.

14

"What is all that over there?" "I'm going to explain, all right? Just wait a second," Flix ordered.

"You are very impatient, young man. Also, curiosity causes trouble!" Flix muttered as he investigated a piece of bark on an old dilapidated tree that could have been sitting there for centuries to now.

Ian figured that Flix was talking and murmuring about him.

"Can you climb?" "Sure," Ian replied.

It took quite some time, but at last they reached the top.

Ian kept worrying the thick branches would snap off.

Flix kept reminding them they wouldn't. Ian hoped that was the case and fact. He couldn't look into the future, anyway.

Flix thought Ian was joking at all this.

Ian got a good look of the battlefield. He quickly scanned it with his eyes. Flix sighed behind him.

"What's going on?" Ian asked politely. He knew non-humans had feelings too. At least he thought they did. Ian could be right or wrong or both.

Tanks were lined up row by row...shooting at enormous *plugs*. It was like a sound booth system.

"Uh, wouldn't they blast each other into pieces...the tanks?" Ian questioned Flix. Flix considered his question for a long stretch of time before answering.

"No...because each has a hole in the back where they can shoot through one. The ammo will just keep flying straight before hitting metal. It's a method to fire at the same time at one target. Do you get it now?" Flix asked.

"Uh, yes, sort of," Ian responded.

"Here, let me clarify this...you see, the one which is at the very front will fire first and the ammo from the tanks behind it will follow. A fact is, our ammo are machines that we program to do something. So in that case, they are playing "follow the leader.""

"Oh-oh-oh…" Ian puffed. "So, how are you do-do-ah?" He fell out of the dilapidated tree and went SMACK on the wet soil ground. Ian felt himself sink into the ground.

Flix had to wrench him out. "Dude that is some weight you've got there!" Ian didn't respond. If he had fell on concrete, his spine might have gotten damaged.

Ian pulled himself up and brushed the soil off his long-sleeves. "What is this wet stuff?" Ian was curious to know. Flix lifted his head. "Molasses!"

"Say that again, I didn't catch the word…" Ian blurted automatically. "Molasses! Do you hear me this time?" Flix asked. "Yeah," Ian replied, a tad less dramatic.

"Ok," Flix changed the topic, "you can't leave this place forever now. You're stuck here with us. There's an invisible electric fence surrounding the boundaries of this island. The only way to escape is by convincing Shadow Clan officials that you are completely innocent," Flix informed Ian.

"Basically, the only way is not a method of escaping, am I right? Why didn't you tell me before my foot hit the nasty ground of this despicable piece of the world?" Ian's voice volume increased.

"Fine," Ian said in a release of carbon dioxide, "where would I drop-off the crystal?" Flix was going to answer, but Ian interrupted him. "Oh no, Joe has it with him! I don't even know where he is…alive or dead!"

Flix seemed nonchalant about the thought Ian shared with him.

Flix waited patiently for several seconds before telling Ian that Shadow Clan had shut down any communication or meeting with humans. Ian was not too surprised and nodded his head a few times.

"I knew they would do that! I knew that would happen and occur!" Ian assured Flix with the matter. "Yup."

They sat in silence at the base of the tree against the trunk. It was wide enough for them to both lean on the same side.

"Oh man…it is not going well over there," Ian pointed out, literally.

Flix shifted his sight and puffed a sigh.

"I've requested them to stop, but as I have repeated to myself…it's no use!" Flix said while looking at the ground.

"Hey, what about you go get a good sleep…oh you can't, never mind," Ian considered. It always helped him to focus after a nice rest. He didn't get why some days he would have positive moods and other times he would have negative ones.

It's just life, Ian thought. Ian understood that Flix was a creature who didn't need to sleep to make energy.

"Um, and also, what are the plugs for?" Ian questioned. Flix responded, "They act like walls when put together, all right?" Ian had to process the fact into his brain for actually a few long seconds.

"Wait, are there any cities in the territory?" Ian asked.

"Yes, two major ones, and many rural towns that aren't safe!" Flix answered, his back straightened.

"Do you have an occupation?" "No, I've been laid-off and kicked-out of being TM." "What's TM?"

"Abbreviated form of Trash Manager, how great is that?" Flix asked. "I worked in Waste Bay!" Flix added.

"Hey, that's not bad! Well, at least you have...I mean, you had a job. What was your monthly pay?"

"Please...don't ask me that question, ok?"

"WE have better things to worry about now, the Shadivil War is not going good...will you help me stop it? I seriously need support," Flix half begged Ian.

Ian looked into his blue dots, they were so familiar, which were eyes.

He thought that being a human was weak, but not in this situation. "Definitely," and that was Ian's ironic answer. It was a wise one too, even though not that smart.

Chapter Three: A Clumsy Attack

Ian was so happy to spot his friends lying on the wet soil next to the freezing sea. He ran to them.

Were they still alive? He thought of this because he didn't see any movement. His grin had become a frown.

Ian was afraid. Was Flix following him? If so, through air or physically? Ian was fearful, he was scared.

They were indeed not-dead. Ian almost shed tears at the sight of them standing up. They were waving at him from a distance.

He tried sprinting farther. His body finally collapsed on the wet soil.

Unlike ShadowClan, Ian needed to conserve energy for everyday life.

He knew this.

Humans were not the same.

Drake was shivering.

Alexis had a red nose.

Reeve's hair was messed-up. Jarret's teeth were chattering.

21

Joe was sputtering and coughing out seawater from his mouth.

He was bent over. Only Blake the Moygeri was there.

"Uh, where's Batelo…?" Ian couldn't finish. "Dead, struck by lightning!" Drake managed to say. Joe looked dismayed. "She was a poor little creature," Alexis shouted. "She didn't deserve the consequence," Alexis added. "Mmhm," Jarret agreed.

"There's too much salt in my beautiful hair!" Reeve complained to the sky. "Why bring me such a punishment?" The others made quickly sure they kept a distance from her. Each stood at least 5 feet from Reeve.

Drake however was at four feet away only.

"Hey! What are you all doing here?" Shadow Clan figures appeared through thin air and hovered over the ground.

"Ah…visitors, I hope!" one said.

They could have jumped back into the sea, but everybody had enough.

Ian remembered every team member just charging at the three creatures who were smiling evilly at them.

Ian went at the middle one, who seemed the biggest of the three. Shadow Clan #1 lifted his metal gigantic foot and flung it somewhere. Ian looked around for it.

The foot unexpectedly hit his bottom-back and he fell down, face-forward. The pain was excruciating…not exciting. Ian couldn't think of anything. He felt like he lost control of his body. Was their going to be a bruise on his lower-back side?

Ian had always known stories about people getting bruises that weren't treated for a long time. They wouldn't care about the injury and later on would die, mostly in their sleep.

His uncle used to say that this was all 'baloney' when Ian was little. He actually believed him numerous times. But since many circumstances and dead-serious storytellers, not so much. He in fact was afraid of getting one nowadays.

There was hardly enough time to recover before a fist came his way.

Ian ducked and dodged immediately.

But then, a knuckle made contact with the bottom of his chin and his head went up. Ian totally wiped-out, his back on the sinking sand, dazed.

He couldn't hear anything.

"Get your body up, you bum!" a Shadow Clan creature called-out.

Ian kicked his feet in the air like he was at the circus.

His Chinese Getups got better during through much practice, so he decided to put it to the test.

It worked, and Ian gave it an A-plus. He was admiring his skill, but for maybe too long. A metal hand pushed his left shoulder backwards, and Ian heard a crack.

All feeling drained from his arm. Another hand punched his knee, and the bone broke into multiple pieces.

Ian was too dizzy to keep it up. He decided that was all the effort needed.

But on the other hand, he'd just lost his shoes and socks somewhere.

Ian was bare-foot and the ground felt worse than freezing.

Did Shadow Clan have veins? He thought curiously.

Then the pain arrived.

Where he had been hit, the skin was sizzling.

Ian's mouth opened wide enough to emit random noises.

His eyes were completely shut.

His face was squeezed together.

Having a no-weapon fight with metal creatures who can travel through air without being seen was hard.

Then Ian felt himself get picked-up into the air and slammed chest-forward onto the ground. It hurt a—lot.

His breathing almost stopped. Were his lungs still going to work correctly? He knew his eyesight just gone out.

Too much fluid and tears built up in both eyelids.

Ian heard his friends all hit the ground with THUDS. They lost the raid.

What would Shadow Clan do to them now? Were they going to be tortured or killed?

"You are all going to a jail with electric bars!" Ian sighed relief.

"Uh, why did you do that, I mean sigh?" Jarret muttered to him, somehow next to Ian so quickly.

"Come on, this is the best way where we are not going to die!" Ian replied.

"I HEAR WORDS!" a Shadow Clan denizen said thoroughly.

Jarret was going to say something back but then went *hush,* which meant he shut his mouth without even a gap to breath air.

"Get up, flesh-sticks!" a different Shadow Clan citizen cried.

As Ian got up obediently, arms raised, he heard Joe utter, "Wow, I sure do love that nickname they dubbed us!"

"No talking!" "Oh—oh, all right, you win, I lose, happy now?" Joe yelled at them.

He was immediately lifted off the ground and slammed into the ground.

Of course it didn't hurt much because of the blackish-brown soil-like stuff, but the force was intense.

Reeve and Alexis watched with their mouths opened. The metal robots chained him to a square-shaped piece of metal.

The chains were humungous.

He was indeed going to be there for a while as they taught him a lesson.

Chapter Four: The Chase

Ian found out that the villages and inhabited places were actually invisible and hovering ten feet above the ground supported by electric beams that somehow keep them floating.

He and his fellow teammates actually had the honor of visiting the First Shadow Clan habitat in mankind history. Was it exciting? I'm not sure. Let's see.

Everything was electrical. Electric burgers, electric offices, electric molasses pools, electric brochures, electric police, electric theatres, electric everything!!

Ian knew that to defeat Shadow Clan, he would need to take away the SOURCE of the electricity.

But where was the source coming from? Did he have the courage to trust these creatures if they ever became allies with humans?

Ian couldn't be the same now. He was far from home and in a foreign land. He has no experience whatsoever. Just face it, Ian thought frustratingly.

The town was a complicated area with a color somewhere between purple and blue rays blasting everywhere.

Ian wondered what would happen if he touched one. Ian knew he wasn't native to the place, so would it hurt?

"This town is cool, man, don't you think?" Drake asked. Ian was shaking all over and was thinking of what was arriving next.

"How do you even like this repulsive place?" Ian thought. "I'm just saying…it's unique," Drake shrugged like it was no big deal. "You know, fear still lingers within me as always," Drake added. "Me too," Ian responded quickly back because a Shadow Clan person was staring straight at them, someone random on the sidewalk of a street.

Suddenly, the whole town's focus was on them only. Somebody was even looking at them far up on a rooftop through binoculars. Ian didn't feel comfortable with this. His friends also stopped in their tracks.

"Which are these?" came from the hoard crowding around now.

Ian wondered how they learned English. And…where was Flix this entire time? Did he abandon them when he had the chance? The thought of this struck Ian like lightning. Flix was gone and not here.

"Ok, time for you all's imprisonment, let's go and see where you guys are going to stay tonight!" the Shadow Clan up front said. He led us to a building in the shape of a, well, rectangular block.

The crowds followed us in.

"Welcome to Syock-Suites!" a lady Shadow Clan informed us.

"Here you will stay for a while and have a great time. Don't worry about the electrical bars, they are for safety. Just, I advise you, don't touch them as far as I and my crew are concerned. Free breakfast in the morning every single day. There is a lounge on the third floor. An outdoor Jacuzzi is on the balcony on the second floor. Don't forget to try our sweet pastries, which are also free!! We hope you enjoy your stay!"

She spoke all this, but Ian only half-heard what she told them. "How do they even do business? I mean, earn good money if everything is free?" Drake questioned.

"Well, maybe their government pays them for this junk. It's like a library, I think," Ian pointed out. Drake considered this. "I don't know, maybe you ARE right," said Drake.

"Why does this building look like a prison? I mean, the outside is all lovely and…," Alexis thought. "Oh my goodness, look at those gigantic nails pinned into the wall!!!"

"Some are through the roof!!" Jarret looked up. "No way, this hotel cannot be 5-stars…" Reeve concluded.

"But guess what, this is not a hotel, it is a 5-star prison house! But if you want to, keep believing that this IS a grand resort," Joe spoke softly.

Joe pointed to a sheet of paper pinned to the bulletin board next to the counter. His finger moved as he struggled to read off it cautiously and slowly.

"Dang, guys, we are screwed," Drake nodded after.

The rest of the day didn't go very well.

Joe was shoved right into a cell without windows and fell asleep after eating a sleeping pill which a guard popped into his mouth with force. Ian and Jarret were pushed into one. And Alexis, Reeve, and Drake had to share another cell.

No daylight shone, only artificial ones through the electric bars.

The inside felt damp and the floor was cold rusty carpet that hasn't been maintained in decades.

There was no sofa or couch to sit on. And obviously, no toilet or bed, which wasn't good for a group of spoiled kids and one middle-aged grown-up who has been living in a free-roaming city ever since been born.

"There is no lamp, TV, bathtub..." Jarret went through a long list as he whined. It was very annoying especially when in a tough circumstance and situation.

The cell was like a room in a dirty tenement.

"Aw...man, I really need to use the bathroom already!" Alexis pointed out to everybody.

"Well, too bad," Drake told her swiftly. "Just, just hold it for some time because that will get you through the day!" Reeve assured Alexis. "But I can't go to sleep with a full bladder!" Alexis whimpered.

"I will ask someone," Ian stood up. Alexis mouthed, *thank you.* "Um, anyone there? I have a friend here who needs to go, like right now!" Ian cried out.

No reply. He tried again, a tad louder. No answer.

Ian was at the verge of a despondency while trying before a gruff and low voice asked, "What's up?" Ian smiled.

Somebody had come and heard him yell.

It was a creature that looked like an ogre. He was big…or even huge in terms of size. He was indeed short for his age.

Alexis went to use the restroom and came back all lively and bright.

Her face glimmered and her happiness came back.

"Hooray!" she said, shaking her Fists. Ian and everyone else applauded softly. "I did it!" Alexis added. Everybody clapped even more and did until their hands got tired.

Finally, the topic of escape came to hand and Ian and his friends discussed without Joe leading it because he was unconscious.

There were no guards or surveillance cameras in sight so they started.

A mission of escape was approved after 15 to 35 minutes of many ideas. There was an air vent in each of their cells, and they were going to climb through them.

They took turns entering the air vent (or tunnel where air dwells).

"What about Joe? He's too heavy to be pulled-up into here," Reeve said when they got up. "Leave him there, we will come back to get him," Ian responded reluctantly.

"What?! No way! We can't do that! That is evil and against what my culture holds and believes!" Reeve flung back.

"It's okay, calm down!" Ian looked away. Sometimes Reeve was a headache for sure. But Drake didn't really see that about her.

34

He was rather day-dreaming about an obvious subject in front of him. His face looked dreamily.

The tunnels were extremely narrow, and they had to squeeze through.

"I'm getting claustrophobic!" Jarret told Ian. "What if the sides of the tunnel push in and tighten around us so we cannot breathe?" Ian didn't reply but did after a while.

"Don't say that, it worries me as much as it might to you! Also, save your energy, please don't talk again!"

Jarret did not and they kept going.

They were going to be stealth ninjas but made much noise.

"I wonder if they would detect a problem in the air vent," Drake joked. "I hope they do not!" Alexis added.

Both of them laughed hysterically at once. Ian couldn't imagine how lovely they would be if as a couple.

Ian was in a hurry to get through the tunnel. It was very uncomfortable in there, he had to admit to his friends.

"Yeah," they corroborated. Ian was feeling trapped.

If you asked Ian if it was exciting, he would answer, "Sort of, what about you try and tell me? I want to know!" He would bounce the ball back to you (not literally).

It was a new experience after all.

Suddenly, somebody turned on the air-conditioning.

Having air blown into your face is supposed to be fun, but not to Ian.

He was the one leading and up front.

"I think they will conclude that the air vents are not working due to a few giant Mole Rats in their vents, hahahaha…." Drake started. Alexis was laughing now.

"Oh, are you laughing your *air* out? Haha…" Drake continued. Ian had to admit that was pretty funny, but couldn't bring himself to laughing as he usually did.

Finally, Ian came across a part where there were three slits in the metal of the tunnel leading to a single room that was pretty small.

Two human beings were actually in there. Ian shook his head and tested his sense of sight to make sure he wasn't imagining or hallucinating. Sure enough, he wasn't doing either.

The two people were talking. Ian did his best to listen.

"Move on! Go! What are you doing?" Jarret asked behind him.

"Shh," Ian hushed back.

Jarret became silent and so as everybody else behind him.

They all listened.

There was a piece of paper on a desk where a bald man was sitting.

It had the map of the world, similar to every other one.

There were arrows drawn all over the world. One of them pointed to Yart, Ian's hometown. He couldn't believe it.

The arrow was drawn with a red Sharpie marker.

What did it mean? There was a legend on the corner of the paper, but it was too far away to be read off.

One of the two men left the room. Ian knew this was the moment.

He gathered up his courage and kicked open the three slit door to the air vent and jumped down onto the table.

The guy was immediately surprised and took his leather belt off.

It was somehow electrical, too. The guy slowly turned into The Shocker. Alexis gasped from above.

"Who's that?" Jarret and Reeve questioned.

"I, only, control Shadow Clan, now give me that crystal of yours!"

"We don't have it!" Ian said back.

"What?!" "Yup, we left it with Joe, who is not with us right at this instance," Drake substantiated from behind Ian.

"Then, you all must die!" The man who left the room came in with muscular arms and legs, The Breaker.

He punched the door and it fell lifelessly onto the ground.

Drake charged and tackled The Breaker, which was not wise.

They rolled all around the floor as they wrestled roughly.

Everybody else hopped down from the air vent. This was going to be a *real* Fight.

"We both will team up and destroy Kakutah as promised!" they cried at the same time. "No, you guys aren't going to!" Ian screamed back. The Shocker went for him. Ian dodged and fell on the ground, sliding.

Jarret got hold of the paper which had a map on it. "Come on, we are leaving through the door, let us go!" Jarret cried.

"Was that a command?" The Shocker questioned as he lifted up a foldable chair to throw at Ian.

Ian did a very good Chinese Getup he was a master at by now and waved at the others to follow him away.

They ran out together.

"Hurry!" Alexis cried into Ian's ear. As they sprinted, the wall and floor behind them were crumbling into multiple sinkholes.

Drake looked back and saw that The Breaker was bashing himself into the wall from one side to the other.

The corridor had a bunch of debris now. The Shocker was all too happy about this.

He kept playing it cool by just moving along the wall in front of The Breaker and not using much effort to catch them quick.

The Shocker didn't even need to try to get Ian's companions.

His tentacles were doing the work. They ran along the wall and some went at them.

Lightbulbs popped overhead, the roof gave in, and the walls disappeared.

Then something happened. Reeve tripped.

"Hey! Reeve fell, we need to help her up!" Drake said breathlessly as he stopped. "Don't care about them, they don't deserve being saved by people like us!" Alexis told Ian. Ian halted. "Why?! Are you kidding me? Stop that! What happened to your good-heartiness?" Ian shook his head in disbelief.

Ian ran back, Jarret at his heels. "Uh, how are we going to rescue...?" Jarret started. "Don't say anything!" Ian flung back.

They were too late. Reeve was already disoriented and Drake...fainted.

The Breaker opened up one hand and collided it with the other which was in a Fist. They met in front of his chest.

"Thanks for coming back!" The Shocker said happily. "I came back only because for a reason!" Ian replied adamantly. Jarret just nodded and backed-away.

Ian's best friend was on the ground just lying there with no clue what was occurring. Ian fought back a tear.

"I will take you two back when possible…" Ian turned back around, so as Jarret. They left hastily.

"You guys will regret that decision of your own!" The Breaker roared.

"Bring the Plan back to us and we won't hurt or harm your companions for at least the rest of the day," The Shocker bellowed loudly. Ian didn't answer to give a signal that meant 'no'. Jarret grinned back at them.

But then, tentacles wrapped around Ian's neck. He was choking.

Jarret tried to pull the thick tentacles away, but they were tough and wouldn't budge. The Shocker was laughing.

"This is the end, Ian Lanterncup, this is the end!!" he yelled.

"No more of you, think of that! My army will hold the world, we will gain control," The Shocker started screaming.

Ian fell on his posterior. "Tickle them!" Jarret whispered.

"Whaaaattt? Nooo way, it's not going to worrk," Ian said. Then he couldn't talk, his face was draining of color.

Jarret's eyes were watering now. Ian couldn't hear now, but saw his mouth moving uncontrollably.

What was he speaking?

"Young boy, there is nothing for you to be able to do. He's gone. Don't bother keep talking to him. He will not rise from the dead, as they always portray that in movies. Come, join us. We are mightier than the government. I'll make you feel at home. I will not push you out of your comfort zone. You will rise up in ranks and become a leader of my army after my death. Consider this, everything you desire in your heart suddenly made real! Now, you must make a choice. There are only two options. Pick…one!" The Shocker told Jarret all this.

Jarret seriously thought of this for a moment.

The Breaker curled his lips.

Ian was dying.

He was.

Then out of the grayness, Alexis came with a few flying and live city-pigeons and they pecked at the tentacles.

The Shocker retreated his tentacles and groaned. Ian broke free.

His senses came back.

Jarret took off. They all did. "Nice job, Alexis," Ian said softly. "Thank you, I'm deeply flattered!" "Now, no fancy words right now!" "Fine, all right."

Ian smiled. "Head this way, kids!" Alexis pointed to a corner.

"Why did you call us kids?" Ian asked. "I felt like I needed to order you two like an adult…you know!" Alexis responded. "Really?" Jarret looked at them.

"Quickly, BURN THE PLAN!" Alexis pointed to a Fireplace.

43

Jarret took the piece of paper out of his pocket and stretched out his hand towards the sickling Fire!

"Just, drop that thing!" Ian told him.

Jarret hesitated.

"Go! Do it or I'll! Give me that! What are you waiting for? Come on! Just toss and throw it in!" Ian blurted.

"I see them!" The Breaker cried. Jarret ran a different direction suddenly.

Ian and Alexis had no choice but to go after him. Where was Jarret going? Why was he doing this?

There was a bright light illuminating from a door at the end of the hallway.

"Over there!" Ian told his friends.

They got there and ran inside.

They appeared in a place full of mirrors where women were putting on cans of makeup and doing their hair.

"Here's the exit!" Alexis pointed out. Jarret lead the way and they exited onto a stage full of actors performing.

They resembled Shadow Clan citizens but Ian wasn't sure if they actually were because of speeding past.

Ian ran into ladies covered in purple jewels several times while Jarret kept pushing men in togas away that were in front of him.

Somebody in the audience even asked the person next to him if we were a part of the show. Alexis dodged all of them easily.

Impressive, Ian thought.

Nice, Jarret thought.

They got off-stage, thankfully and headed for daylight.

This time, Alexis lead the way through the side aisle to the emergency exit door. It flung open at her touch of hand.

Ian found himself on a cobblestone street. Jarret looked confused. "Where are we?" he questioned. "No time to answer, we need to seek refuge!" Alexis replied.

She went in a maze, going this way and that. Ian lost track of where they came from. Jarret kept calling out the different street names to remember where they started.

"How come there isn't electric bolts flying around here?" Jarret thought for a second. "Oh yeah, I really have no clue!" Alexis cried out over the wind. "Ah! The sunlight is blasting me!" Ian complained.

Then the weather kicked in. Electricity was everywhere again. "Oh man, I don't like the feeling of this!" Jarret pointed out.

"Oh, why does it have to be like this?" Alexis agreed.

Then they got out of town, somehow. Miles of blackish-brown soil came into view. "Hide, guys," Alexis told them.

"But how? There aren't any hills to hide behind!" Ian asked.

"Dig yourself into the ground and…you know, cover yourself with the dirt, or whatever you want to call it," Alexis told him. Jarret nodded his agreement. "Yup, I think that is the best choice we have so far," he said.

So they did for the night.

Chapter Five: The Rescue Mission

The sun rose high the next morning, but it was obscured by clouds that emitted lightning bolts.

"Is there a map in the region, I mean, anywhere on this piece of land?" Jarret brought up. "How do I know?" Alexis responded frustratingly. "We hardly know anything about this place," Ian continued.

"Do you think they are watching us?" Alexis asked Ian.

"Yeah, sure…" "I'm hungry!" Jarret said. "Will you please stop?" Alexis cried back at him. "Hey…calm down now…" Ian moved his hands in circles.

"Yeah, I am pretty sure there aren't any maps because they can just travel through air to anywhere they want without needing any directions, hey, it's a theory!" Jarret told Alexis, trying to calm her nerves. It sort-of worked because she didn't talk back. Ian stepped between them to reduce the chances of a physical Fight between them.

"Is there any human-edible food around here?" Ian wondered. Alexis didn't respond. "Well, maybe!" Jarret said, trying to lift both of their hopes up.

"What I really need now is fresh water, not salt water," Jarret told Ian.

"Yeah, me also," Ian said back.

Then something occurred, rain.

"Yes, our hopes have been made real!" Ian and Jarret said at almost the same time.

It actually started showering and then pouring.

Suddenly, enormous trunks rose from all around.

Venus flytraps shot out from the soil and went all the way to 30 feet high.

"We should better get moving!" Alexis suggested.

But then, they lost the sight of the sky and were now stuck in a forest of some kind. Fog glistened around. "This is scary," Jarret muttered to Ian.

Were they losing it? Blurry images came into view, feet from them.

Ian felt like he kept attempting to wake up from a nightmare, but it would keep dragging his consciousness back into its own thing.

Then music erupted. Loud music. His ears couldn't take it.

Then he had to face the fact that he wasn't leaving this place.

The Mist was present. The Haunter was nearby.

Then something said, "Let go of your pain, don't try to endure it. Burden is hard, just let it slip through the gaps between your Fingers. It will be gone. Think of this, milk leaving your hand. It's as easy as that."

Ian couldn't see his friends nor himself. His head was spinning.

Ian was on bended knee.

He knew this was a trickster talking to him. He would have to suffer even more if he let go of his burden.

It wasn't true, the words whoever spoke. It was worth the effort to not lose his grip on his burden.

Ian blindly and slowly stood up and let loose a meaningless sound from his mouth.

"I will not let go of my burden!" he concluded.

His focus suddenly went on a tree trunk. There were words carved on it. A letter. There was a message written on it.

It was a ransom note.

To whom left their friends,

I am the head of the Shadow Clan territory and I want to let whoever is reading this and his companions to please read carefully and mindfully what I wrote below,

Tonight at 7:00pm, turn yourself in and we shall trade with each other. The Plan and the Lost Crystal for the hostages, okay? None of your teammates will die if the deal is approved. If late half an hour, all of our captives will be put to the sword. See you later. Arrive at 639840512 Willows Lane, City Yellow. Good Luck.

50

"This can't be! How did Drake, Reeve, and Joe end up in the hands of Shadow Clan?" Ian thought.

"Well, didn't The Shocker say he controlled Shadow Clan? So maybe they have them right now," Jarret answered. Alexis still looked dazed and trying to concentrate after the mysterious encounter.

"Um, who has the crystal?" Ian asked after several seconds.

"I do," Alexis said, opening her duffel bag. "Good," Jarret told her. "I thought we left it with Joe, where it would have been still attached to the staff…" Ian smiled.

"If that was the case, we would have been really dumb for forgetting such an important item!" Jarret pointed out.

"Yeah," Alexis agreed.

"Jarret, do you still have the Plan in your pocket?" Ian asked.

"Yup, no need to worry," Jarret responded.

"Hey, I found some subs!" Alexis cried, digging into her bag.

She took out a couple that were still wrapped in plastic.

"Are you sure they haven't gone bad, already?" Jarret questioned.

"I think they are okay, just taste it to be sure," Alexis assured him.

Ian took a bite.

His stomach suddenly felt satisfied. It no longer growled.

His liveness came back. Yes, he thought.

But then, a silhouette appeared on the thin grass. Ian looked up.

One of the Venus Flytraps were staring at them with its tongue out in the open. It was a fairly long tongue and curved ten feet down. The weird thing was: it hopped out of the soil and *waddled* towards them.

"RUN!" Ian screamed and yelled. He dropped his sandwich. Jarret and Alexis followed him as he took off. "This duffel bag is extremely heavy!" Alexis said. "Here, I will take it…" Ian took the duffel bag from Alexis who reluctantly lent it to him.

Other Venus Flytraps hopped out of the soil behind them, and dodged trees. "Are they trying to eat us?" Jarret asked. "I don't know, but I think so!" Ian replied.

Not much light shone from the canopy. The forest was almost pitch black.

It was dark, and slamming into tree trunks wasn't Ian's thing.

The Venus Flytraps must have had eyes with good night vision.

But their eyes weren't even visible.

Then Ian remembered that they used their sense of smell instead.

Oh, he thought.

After a few minutes, Alexis said, "Clear land in the distant!"

It was all flat land.

"I see a city ahead!" Jarret called out.

Suddenly, trees starting toppling over each other. Ian put his hands over his head as he jumped over fallen tree trunks.

It was past noon now.

"I need to take a break from running…" Alexis said.

"No, you can't, they…" Ian started. "Actually, I believe we lost them," Jarret interrupted.

So that was where they stopped to take a rest from sprinting for their lives.

But then, the ground gave way, and they fell into a ditch.

It wasn't deep, but they couldn't climb up to leave the ditch.

They needed a ladder, but there just wasn't one.

"This is terrible, we are going to be stuck here and when those Venus Flytraps discover that we are here and cannot leave, they will…" Alexis started.

"No, don't keep on going," Ian pleaded with her. She just nodded in return.

Jarret attempted to run up the side of the ditch.

He boosted himself by running from the other side. But it back-fired.

His foot went on the side, and he clawed at the edge above him.

But his foot poked a hole in the side and Jarret got stuck for good.

More of the ground slid into the ditch. Ian and Alexis had to cover their faces because of the dirt that got into the air.

Jarret fell backwards, and Ian heard an ugly crack. "Oh, are you okay?" Alexis asked, running to Jarret.

It was a common respond. "Yeah, yeah," Jarret replied.

"Dude, it could be serious," Ian told his cousin. "Well, I don't know about that, but there isn't a hospital or medical center that is even friendly to humans around here, I'm pretty sure, so…" Jarret answered.

"I feel bad for you, man," Ian told him. "Thanks…" Jarret said back, still drowsy, trying to concentrate.

Alexis was hugging him all over. Ian wished Alexis was doing that to *him,* somehow. He didn't know why, himself. It was a sudden desire, nothing he would expect at all.

Then Ian had an intelligent idea. "Alexis, I have something to tell you. What about we take clumps of dirt to shape into blocks so after they dry up, they would be the steps of a staircase? I mean, it's just like making brick to walk up on," Ian informed her.

"But that will take hours, and how are we going to shape the dirt into separate blocks?" Alexis questioned.

"Um, uh, let me think," Ian started. "Good question by the way." Alexis nodded her head like she was proud of herself.

Pride, Ian thought.

So they took a whole chunk of time to make 4 blocks using Alexis' duffel bag, after she took everything out.

It actually worked. By the time they were finished, it was 3pm already.

"Wow, we used like the entire day," Jarret piped in. "Come on, you didn't even help us," Ian said to him. "Yup," Alexis substantiated.

"Time to place!" Ian exclaimed, trying to look like he was excited, rubbing his hands together.

Jarret took Block #1 and went over to the side of the ditch. He dropped it, and the dirt scattered on the ground. Ian was horrified. Alexis looked like she was going to die.

"Why did you do that?!" Ian screamed. "We took like 2 hours to make even only one!" he added. Alexis couldn't say anything. She was too shocked.

"Get out of my sight! Behind me! Over there! I don't want to see you again!" Ian yelled at his cousin.

"How could you do this?" he added, still yelling. "That was a waste! We burned much effort on that! We used our heart! We…" Ian stopped. Jarret did what he told him to do obediently.

"I'm sorry…I'm sorry for yelling at you," Ian said sympathetically, glaring at the ground. "I'm just distraught, or tired, or exhausted," Ian exclaimed.

"Just, sometimes, I think you are very annoying…I just cannot handle it as well as others might," Ian trailed off. "My tolerance is limited, unlike others," he admitted.

"It's all okay, I forgive you, really, for serious," Jarret answered. He still wasn't looking at Ian as he always has.

"Yeah, all that has happened today really got my head spinning. I need self-control. I need temper management, for real," Ian told his cousin. He pursed his lips.

The stairs were set by the time the sun was about to set…and the electricity was coming back. "Ready!" Alexis said.

Jarret went up, but then started running away as fast as possible from Ian. "What are you doing? Come back!" Ian yelled.

"Just let him wander and roam," Alexis told him. "He will eventually come back…"

Jarret by then had disappeared in the woods. There were only several footprints in the mud to show which direction he ran towards.

So Ian and Alexis headed for the city in the distance. They had to stop a few times.

Then they saw it. There was a ginormous *thing* in the middle that had an indistinct shape. Plugs were attached to the top of whatever the *thing* was. They curved downwards, and kept plugging itself on the road. Ian didn't know why, obviously.

As they got closer, Ian realized that the plugs transported Shadow Clan Figures by taking just one into itself, retracting to the sky, and then landing on someplace different to release the Shadow Clan citizen.

Cable wires were like the necks, and the plugs were like the heads.

"Here's a coat to cover your identity…" Alexis gave one to Ian.

"What about you?"

"Oh, I have one myself too," she replied. So they put them on.

There were hoodies, so they lifted them up onto their heads.

City Yellow was full of flyers and billboards criticizing the other city.

They were everywhere. Some up high, others in the lower part.

"How are we going to signal a plug to come get one of us?" Ian asked.

"Move closer," Alexis whispered back.

They did. Shadow Clan citizens walked all around them.

Some even stopped as they passed by, which got Ian nervous.

Finally, they got within 25 feet of where the plugs were attached to. It was a huge warehouse that was covered with dark paint. The windows were cracked.

"I think this *is* the place," Alexis pointed out. "You sure?" Ian asked.

"Yeah, look at that plate..." "Oh, right," Ian said.

"Wait..." POOM! "Where are we?" Ian cried suddenly.

"I think it's one of those plugs, you know," Alexis responded.

Then a mechanical lady's voice erupted.

"Destination? Who are you two?" it spoke. Ian tried to mimic Flix. "Shadow Clan, of course." Alexis nudged him. "Don't say of course, it's very suspicious!" she whispered.

"Oops!" Ian answered too quickly.

"What was that? Checking body weight, please, a moment...wow, what a skinny couple, why is their blood on you, Shadow Clan?" "You mean in me?" Ian thought. "Yes." "Don't talk!" Alexis almost yelled at him.

"Operation aborted, sending suspicion to head-of-industry..." it started.

"No!" Alexis screamed.

Then, before they knew something was going to happen, darts collided with the glass panels that were windows at the sides of the plug.

It sounded like ping-pong for a few seconds. "It's ok, they won't break through..." Ian assured Alexis.

But he was wrong.

The entire front window shattered. Chips and pieces of glass fell.

One went right into Ian's right knee.

Ian groaned in pain. Alexis was shielding herself in a tornado-safety form at the far corner. Other windows were shot down and crumbled to the floor.

Then, miraculously, the plug started to ascend towards the sky.

Ian's joy only lasted for a second before the entire plug blew up and disintegrated, leaving them both to plunge from a height of any kind.

Somehow, they stopped in mid-air. Somebody was grasping their ankles. Ian and Alexis were pulled into somewhere they didn't know.

It was Flix all over again.

"Okay, they are bound in iron chains on the bottom level.

We are going to snatch them and not hand over the crystal, good?"

"Are you two with me?" he asked.

"Why did you leave us? I mean, Jarret's gone now," Ian thought.

"Here, you have got to come see this…" Flix said.

Ian went over to the railings and looked down below.

The cable wires of the plugs were all in their separate holes but were all tied together to a furnace the size of half the Empire State Building's length.

"Okay, you know what powers the plugs? Human flesh, believe it or not.

So if we don't save the others in time, they will become fuel, like gas is to car."

Flix was playing it human now.

He descended the stairs one step at a time to the bottom level.

Ian and Alexis followed.

"Hide behind this crate and barrel…" Flix told them. "I'm going to try something out," he added.

"Okay," they replied reluctantly.

"Let this operation stop at this instant!" Flix yelled at the plugs.

They slowed down. "That's well enough," he muttered. "Come out, it's safe, we are going to get you friends," he said.

It felt like a factory, all damp.

"Guys, Drake, Reeve, Joe, are you injured?" Alexis ran to them.

Ian saw that they were fast asleep.

They were sprawled on the ground, still all tied up.

A wheel kept on moving next to them, and it was dragging them towards the furnace. "We need to prevent..." Ian started.

"I know, I know, but this will not be as easy as you might think," Flix informed him.

He tried to yank a chain from Joe but it just tightened its grip on him.

Then after some thinking, Flix took out something that looked like a saw-gun from within his belly.

"This can only be used once," he said. Flix broke each chain into quarters with a very serious concentrating facial expression. One false move, and...

Finally, the captives broke free, each and every one of them.

Flix pushed them together and hugged them. He then Shadow-Travelled out of the warehouse. Where was he taking them? Was it a place that was harmless?

"Ian!" that shook him back to awareness. The roof was crumbling bit by bit.

"Flix shoved his saw-gun into the moving wheel! We need to go and leave right now!" Alexis cried.

"Escape through the window, or chimney," Ian yelled.

"The chimney's blocked, leave through the window!" Alexis screamed.

Stacks of brown cardboard boxes on shelves kept tumbling down.

"Hurry, we will be squashed!" Alexis yelled.

An alarm went off.

They ran up to the second floor. A part of it broke off and went swinging.

Ian almost fell off. "Here!" Alexis pointed.

"We can't reach that high up! Is there a ladder?" Ian asked.

Alexis brought one over and climbed out. "Now we jump!" she said.

Ian and Alexis took hands without second thought (or blushing) and jumped down. It was indeed a life-or-death situation.

While they were doing that, the entire warehouse exploded behind them.

Ian could feel the heat scrape his back.

Chapter Six: Tunnel of Fear

Ian arose in the dark, on a half-paved road in the wilderness. The blast and gust of air from it had thrown him into the tree land and Circular Park around the main city.

Shadow Clan citizens surrounded him and where he landed, some were holding signs reading "Our-People Supremacist" and "Do not Even Think of Preventing Us from What We Wanna Do!" Ian's personal opinion was that the message was a tad too long and not concise. Then he was jabbed and slapped in the hips.

A Shadow Clan in a red glow in the dark jacket stood over him, taller. Ian tried getting on his tippy-toes to try to be leveled with the guard and face his face, but it did not work. Ian was an entire head lower than him.

"Level with me, what is the main motive concerning that you are here? Our city council has watched your every move…" the red-jacket man questioned seriously.

"Listen, hard boiled bimbo! Do you think you are a cop or what?" Ian asked with a tone of toughness. He was getting the heebie-jeebies. "But I am!" the red-outfit citizen told him. Shadow Clan around them made "burn!" noises.

Ian was still sitting on the ground, and so the policeman cried, "Get on your dogs!" Ian scrambled up in less than 2 seconds.

"Now, hear me, rag-a-muffin, I need the truth from you and if you do not give it to me in time, or ever, you are so…"

"Hey partner, I found this girl lying on the plains over there," another red jacket citizen walked out of the darkness.

"I wonder…" the bimbo who had been talking to Ian looked back at him. "You know this dame?"

"Uh-uh, yes, I do," Ian replied. The Shadow Clan man started laughing so hard his red jacket came off. "I—do? Haha!" Ian did not know what was so funny.

"Human! You are stuck on this tomato! It is about time you will buy a handcuff for…" Ian was infuriated and jittery.

"I have had an earful of your baloney that is all you are going to razz about!" Ian ran and broke through the crowd, bumping his fingers and cracking knuckles.

Ian felt angry at getting hurt. He shook his hand to get away the pain.

Ian did not know where he was heading or going. He decided to run away aimlessly, maybe live in the wild.

Ian went around a corner and ran into the former captives, his friends. "Oh, Ian, I failed you by passing out!" Reeve hugged him right on spot. Joe walked towards them from behind. "Hey, um, where is Alexis?"

"She is at a place that is safe, and harmless," Ian lied, looking at the ground. Joe didn't sense anything was wrong somehow.

Then, out of the blackness, the same not people persons seized Drake, each gripping one of his arms.

"Let's go," one of them told the other. They ran, dragging along Drake. "It is those Shadow Clan guys that I really and very hate much! Get them!" Ian yelled.

His friends seemed loath to start getting on the move again. "Well, so?" Joe then led the group and off they went.

"Just follow them!" Ian shouted.

They sprinted at the beginning, but then slowed down gradually.

Ian was sweating and moving his arms back and forth with much effort and strength. This was like testing your cardiovascular endurance back in PE, the class he was only so-so at.

Ian spotted a sign reading "No Citizens beyond This Point or You Will Surely Never Leave!" Then they entered a cave-like tunnel down into the ground.

The walls were made of pyro clast.

An arch shaped like half a circle jutted from the ceiling.

The middle of the walls on both sides came in. The entire complex was pure neon blue, at least from inside.

Joe went in before any of them could. Everyone took turns and slid in. They ran on the transparent walkway.

Steel bars held it up on either sides. A three feet gap was on both sides of the walkway to the walls.

Ian looked down and saw lava underneath, about a twenty-foot drop. The glass had cracks in it and did not look stable. Also, there were no railings.

They followed Drake's frantic cries.

69

Ian saw that his shirt was ripped-off entirely. The guards hoisted him up and started marching quickly from a distance toward a big door with a lock on the front side.

"Hurry!" Reeve called.

Up ahead was a machine that had two metal slaps coming together and also getting apart. It kept doing the same thing.

The guards easily took out a device that looked like a remote control and stopped it for them to pass before turning it on again. Oh boy, Ian thought.

"We need to slide through that thing at the right exact time!" Joe cried. They got to it and he went...successful.

One by one sliding through it before getting squashed.

Ian was the last, and he wasn't sure if he wanted to take the risk. "Um, I think I will stay here for you guys," Ian hesitated. "Come on, is this like saving the world?" Joe asked. "No..." "Then just go for it!"

Ian dove through, but the bottom of his pants got stuck. Ian pulled. Joe and Reeve rushed to help, and together...yeah!

"See? Easy job!" Joe gave a thumbs-up. Reeve nodded.

Ian shook his head.

They continued running. Ian thought of Jarret, and how he made the right decision to just leave them.

It was better than being here. But on the other hand, he might be in danger even though he wasn't in the same situation.

What was next?

Ian looked at the end of the tunnel. There was a door with a lock. He shook his head and looked away.

When he eyed the door again, it still seemed like the exact distance from them than when he checked.

Ian blinked several times as he took a few more steps.

This time, he knew something was wrong. No matter how much they ran, the door wasn't getting any closer.

Keep going, he thought.

Then the walls were coming together on both sides.

Ian stopped and looked around. The ceiling lowered.

The twenty-foot bottom seemed as though it was rising. The lava sizzled, and some flung up and burned the top of the glass walkway. Ian jumped in fear.

Then, the locked door acted like a train coming right at them, flying their way instead of getting lengthier. Where they had come from suddenly bounced up and flew towards them from behind. Reeve looked terrified. Joe looked horrified.

The tunnel was shrinking. "This cannot be real, it is an illusion," Reeve repeated several times.

The air became thick, harder for them to breath.

Ian felt himself suffocate.

"Ian! Ian! Guys! Close your eyes and think as though none of this is real. Do not get claustrophobic! Spread out! Move around! Feel as though it is roomy here! Go!" the voice of Reeve cried.

Was she even trustable? Could the voice be a guidance?

Ian couldn't remember a thing after that. He was sprawled on the glass. Joe lifted him up. "Dude, it is almost over," he said.

Ian regained self-consciousness. When Reeve saw him, she gave him a grin. "Ok, where were we, why are we here, what now?" Ian questioned. "Follow our lead, the memory is blurry in me too, but come on..." Joe snapped, heading forward.

The door with the lock was in front of them. "There's a keyhole!" Ian pointed out. "Don't worry, I have the key, or one of them," Joe showed it. It was bronze-colored, and mostly made of copper.

"How did you get that?" Ian asked. "Oh, pick-pocketed one of those Shadow Clan guards. Very fortunate that I got it, wasn't too easy," Joe answered.

But there was something different. "Why are there like 3 rings of electricity?" Ian saw and showed them. "Oh...yeah," Reeve nodded. Joe looked confused.

Joe carefully inserted the key. He had to make sure it didn't touch any of the electric rings floating in the air.

For a moment, Joe's hand shook, and the key came close into contact with the last ring closest to the lock. "What is this, some sort of security?" Ian thought.

Reeve let out a sigh of relief. The tip of the key stopped at a centimeter away from the edge of the ring.

"Why is everything electrical? It's like farther into the future!" Joe thought to himself and asked particularly to no one. The door clicked and opened by itself.

Chapter Seven: The Deal

Ian thought the door opened by itself, but actually didn't. Ian walked in and appeared in a place three times larger than an auditorium. Shadow Clan sat in every seat there was. Delegate seats extended in a semi-circle from one side to the other. Two balconies were in the back. Each row of seats was a step higher.

Drake was in an old couch next to the door. He looked sleepy.

Ian realized that he, Reeve, and Joe were the center of attention in the Shadow Clan territory right there.

This must be the Council Committee of Shadow Clan Worries.

It resembled what the UN main building in New York looked like.

"Welcome, trouble-makers, we are here to resolve the problem with you people…" a Shadow Clan woman with glasses spoke on a podium attached to the stage, covered with very brown and dark green carpet.

"Hey, what's up?" Ian winked, giving his humor a shot. Since touching this piece of land, he wasn't able to implement sarcasm.

"That is highly disrespectful and not acceptable," the same woman said. "You will face consequences if after a second time, have I made myself clear?"

"Take a seat here!" the woman spoke smoothly, like she wanted to keep the procedure going.

Ian, Reeve, and Joe formally sat down next to a table with a piece of tarp and a cloth draped over it.

This was all a set-up. The guards took Drake as bait to lead them here.

"Now…give us the truth!" the woman Shadow Clan cried.

A delegate rose in his seat way above the center stage. "I believe and sense a very valuable item in one of their possessions," he announced to everyone.

Joe took out his staff from behind him. It was a mop before.

The crystal shone with a sparkle that triggered Shadow Clan's emotions. It was purple, and everybody wanted it.

All of Shadow Clan was staring at, or at least eyeing the crystal.

"Now, humans, what can we do to regain this crystal?" the woman citizen asked. Ian stood up and started talking.

"I have heard this here is a symbol of friendship for centuries, and my team and I have brought it today, through a treacherous journey to lend this back to you guys. I hope for the best and friendship between our races. I believe this will stop strife and conflict. Here is the question, will you, Shadow Clan, accept this gift?" Ian sat back down, looking serious.

"Very convincing and compelling!" Joe whispered to him.

"We will…if there is another favor done!" the woman responded.

By that time, Ian felt so angry he could burst. His blood boiled. Another favor? Wasn't that all they wanted?

"Fine, what is the favor?" Reeve stood up this time.

"It is fairly an easy one to take, and it is for your race to work together with City Yellow to attack and bring down the opposite side of this civil war," she spoke.

"We are the government and we need to regain territory lost to them. City Yellow is the ruler of this continent and is in control!" the woman added.

"Oh, I am not sure because I would need to consult with our own government before deciding upon your desire. Sending our own troops into war with you guys is very radical," Reeve replied with intelligence.

"Too bad! This deal must be set and concluded today, or you humans will never leave this place!" Some Shadow Clan citizens spoke into their little microphones that curved upward in an arch, extending from their long desks that sat several of them in each row.

"Ok, let's settle the deal," Ian answered. Joe said, "Yeah," to corroborate.

"All right, it is passed!!" the lady Shadow Clan looked back at a piece of odd-appearing paper on her podium.

"Now, let us go!" Joe stood up. "I am sorry, but you cannot!" all the Shadow Clan started chanting.

There was an exit at the back, but was too far away.

They would have to go through all those Shadow Clan to escape.

"Guys, hold onto each other, and we are zipping away from this place!" Ian smirked and shot out his grappling hook.

"Hey! Stop them!" a Shadow Clan with a deep voice shouted.

The crystal left with them. Ian knew it was a prized possession. He didn't want to leave it there, but keep it instead.

They zipped through the air and got to somewhere safe.

But the only thing Ian was not expecting was doing a careless job. He smacked into something solid and hard.

Chapter Eight: Wanted

Ian awoke. Where was he at?

Flix looked at him from above. "Hi," he told him and said.

"Will you tell me what I don't know?" Ian questioned.

Flix sighed. "No!"

"What? Why?" Ian didn't expect that answer.

"We have to get out of the Shadow Clan territory. They are not going to accept the crystal as an act of friendship. It's too late. The Haunter has already controlled them. They have sent me a message," Flix said.

"No way, but we went and travelled so far from our homes! This can't be!" Ian cried, he was on the verge of crying.

"I'm deeply sorry, but this is the truth," Flix answered.

"Where are the others?" Ian asked. "Oh, under the blue tent outside," he replied. "Are they recovering?"

"Yeah, there are only minor injuries," Flix responded.

"What time is it?" Ian asked.

"About 4 or 5 in the morning," Flix said. "Wow, I actually slept?" "Yup!"

"How far are we from the border line?" "A hundred miles, my Shadow-Locator tells me," Flix responded. "Oh man."

"Come on, we are leaving!" Flix said.

They walked towards the sea and kept avoiding populated towns.

Couple times, they almost got into bad circumstances.

Finally, the shoreline came into view.

Ian found Jarret swimming in the cold water. Was he trying to freeze himself? Ian thought. Anyway, he was very happy to see him again. Who knows what would have happened?

Jarret was a big target indeed.

"Follow me, there is a ferry boat off the coastline…" Flix said.

They got on it and Flix went to the steering wheel.

There were many seats and a deck on the top for sightseeing.

"Bye, Shadow Clan territory!" they all said except Flix, and the boat flowed into the bay. "We are heading to Kakutah, which is north," Flix told all of them.

"One more question, why were there no Shadow Clan citizens inside the warehouse at that time?" Ian asked.

"Oh, because we were early!" Flix told him.

"One more thing, I want to let you guys know that we are all wanted, including me!" Flix told everybody aboard.

PART TWO:
THE WAY HOME

Chapter Nine: Shipwreck

"Was all that a dream? It was crazy!" Drake exclaimed after they lost sight of the territory. "Guys, we are in grave danger, they are going to hunt us down beyond their borders," Flix told them.

Then somehow, the ship stopped moving. "Flix, what are you doing?"

"Nothing! I'm just trying to make the ferry boat go! It won't budge!" he replied.

"Come, there is something wrong here..." Reeve pointed out.

Ian walked over and peeked over the side.

There was a gap in the ship, and gas was leaking out of it.

"I'm not sure if that's the source at all, but..." Reeve started.

"Hey, hey, it has to be!" Joe strode over. "Uh, anyone have tape?"

"You are cheap, man, we all know that's not going to work very well," Drake informed Joe. "How do you know?" he asked back.

"Is this some kind of humor?" Drake questioned. "No! I mean tape isn't as bad as you think," Joe cried.

"Are you kidding me? It's terrible on metal pieces," Drake said back.

"Guys, don't panic or argue, we can solve the problem as a team, am I right?" Alexis told them two.

They continued to argue with different opinions of tape.

First, they yelled at each other about tape, then it went to how calculators were beneficial and harmful after Drake said, "My mind is as smart as a calculator, but yours is not!"

They cried and screamed over each other until their spit flew all over the place. Then the topic and subject was changed to who was stronger.

Suddenly, they started physically punching each other.

Drake crushed Joe very badly. Joe kept gagging on the floor as Drake stood over him and slapped his face.

Then Drake retreated and said, "I will let you have one more try, get up, come at me!" Joe pushed himself up and charged.

He took Drake's legs and flung him over boat.

"That's enough!" Ian shot in. "We need to conserve our energy for later use!"

Flix seemed unaware of all this. He was whistling to himself.

Then he stopped.

"I heard a rustle!" Flix looked Ian straight in the eye. Ian's heartbeat halted.

Sloogpaps hopped from the deck above onto them and they were taken down to the floor. "Get off me!" Jarret cried. Blake the Moygeri ran towards Flix while wailing.

Flix scooped him up and set him on his shoulder.

The ferry boat was sinking quickly. "We need...to keep the ship balanced!" Ian managed to say as he struggled to make the Sloogpap loosen its grip on him.

It did and he broke free.

But his friends weren't too lucky.

"Get the survival vests, anybody!" Ian cried. Flix kept Shadow-Travelling out of the Sloogpaps' ways with Blake on his shoulder.

Water rose to Ian's ankles. "Move to the top!" he shouted.

As Ian climbed up the stairs, the boat tilted and lurched.

Ian was thrown to the floor beneath him. His back hurt.

The ferry boat creaked and cranked. The hull was pretty much destroyed.

The engine was absorbing water.

Ian couldn't think of anything else that mattered to him but the pain.

His limbs went limp.

Then the ferry boat exploded from within. The steam pole cracked in half and dove into the sea with the help of gravity.

Some Sloogpaps fell off the ship, which was a good thing.

"Get together, come on," Flix told everybody else.

They huddled together and disappeared into the shadows as the entire ferry boat went down sideways and slammed the water.

Chapter Ten: The Miles-Long Tunnel

They appeared on a courtyard of some sort where flowers were growing.

Honeybees zigzagged in the air around them. Drake gagged. "I'm allergic to bees!!" he said and ran away as far as could until meeting the shoreline.

"Uh, where's the city?" Jarret asked. "Oh, in front of you..." Flix answered.

A building rose in front of them. The pillars that supported the roof were marble.

They stood with a helix shape, which surprised Ian very much.

Thick bluestone was on the ground for them to step on.

The roof of the building wasn't triangular, but somehow caved in on the top.

What would happen if snow piled up?

There were no windows, and the building seemed to extend in many miles.

Ian couldn't see where it ended. It seemed to go on forever.

"This cannot be the city, you're lying, it's a jailhouse, I mean, and it even looks like one!" Jarret cried. "Fine, believe me or don't believe me, there?" Flix replied and turned away.

"Uh, where's the entrance?" Ian questioned. "I hope I didn't get it wrong but I think it is the roof!" Flix told him.

"First of all, um, how are we going to get up there?" Alexis asked.

"Climb! Do you not know how to?" Flix said back.

"Yeah..." she responded. "No way, that can't be," Flix replied. "It is the truth though," Alexis answered. "Okay, I will lift you up there but you owe me."

"Sure," Alexis said.

Flix pushed her up through the air but then landed on the side where the wall was.

Then he let go of and left her at two tiny notches where her feet were on.

"Flix! Come back here, I'm going to kill you!" Alexis screamed, not daring to look at the ground nor even open her eyes.

"Why would I? Make me!" Flix replied.

90

He chuckled in his machine-like manner. Ian missed hearing that.

"Let her at least try to get up there," Flix told them.

"It's worth the experience..." he added. "Agreed!" Reeve cried loudly.

Drake came back over with his face covered in salt water.

"This will protect me from getting stung!" Drake told them.

"I'm not too sure about that, you know..." Reeve complimented.

"Why is Alexis all the way up there?" Drake pointed out. "She is just having some fun," Reeve answered.

So they climbed. Finally, they got to the top. "Ok, here's the tough part," Flix announced. "You will have to slide-down headfirst..." he said. Ian looked at his friends and boy were they confused. "Yes, that's what you have to do to enter the city of Kakutah!" Flix substantiated.

"Won't we get hurt, because that is some serious concrete down there..."Alexis asked, raising her hand.

"Have faith, Alexis, it will work!" Flix replied. "Wait, so the line where the halves of the roof meet would open up?" Jarret asked. "Of course, yup, you got it right!"

"I'm so diving in!" Drake went down, and then before it looked like he was going to hit the rooftop, he just vanished.

They took turns and then it was only Flix, Joe, and Ian.

"I'm not sure about this," Joe whimpered.

"I told you, have faith! Do you know what faith is? You can even have faith in a chair to support your rear end!" Flix cried out loud. "Oh, okay," he went and disappeared.

"Ian, you go..." Flix said, looking at him. "What? No! I don't want to lose you again..." Ian said back.

Flix dove downwards and was out of sight. Ian took his time up there.

Then Ian went, and he was gone.

Ian then appeared again.

He was flying through the sky downwards. Ian went straight into clouds, drips of water shimmering on his cheeks.

Whiteness blurred his view, and Ian was forced to shut his eyes.

The ground came into view, and Ian was starting to get scared and afraid.

He'd sky-dived once before and was screaming.

Ian's anxiety rose as he got closer to the ground. Skyscrapers rose from the metropolitan area. It looked like he was going to fall on an antennae and get pinned to death.

On the other hand, did it hurt, and was it painful to go SMACK on the road beneath? If so, was he going to die immediately or suffer for a few seconds? These questions popped into Ian Lanterncup's head.

The wind felt good. Maybe he was already dead!

Ian looked at the orange-purple sunset and smiled.

His face was warmed up from the cold air he came from.

Somehow, Ian didn't feel the same. He felt like he was underwater and looking up at a city with beautiful lights.

Ian had a feeling of euphoria. He was finally at peace with that feeling he loved. It was better than eating his favorite food.

Ian felt like he didn't have anything to worry about anything, with zero challenges coming his way he would have to face. Ian was so comfortable that he felt drowsy physically. He was falling asleep.

What is happening?

Ian suddenly knew he had to resist the temptation.

He was falling asleep in midair! Ian told himself to try to wake up.

There was nothing to joke about now. This was a test, he thought.

Then a bomb exploded somewhere. He heard it but couldn't see the smoke that supposedly should be billowing into the air.

Ian smelt it, and suddenly he couldn't feel his own body. Everything went limp. Ian realized he was a rag or a piece of cloth getting pushed by gravity towards its landing point.

This was the worse option of dying. Was he dead already?

Ian would never know since he couldn't hear nor touch or see anymore. His sense of smell was still there, but it was no use. In fact, it was slowly dying away.

This was horrible.

Then his senses came back, Ian was on an inflatable mattress. He realized he was wheezing heavily. "Take him to the ER!" a stranger cried to somebody else. Ian felt himself get lifted up into the trunk of an ambulance.

$$* * *$$

"So, what kind of gadget do you have there, huh, it looks expensive," the doctor said. Ian opened his eyes in a moderate speed. "Oh…hi, don't bother stealing it," Ian stared at the ceiling. "No, not that, I just want to know what that is!" the doctor called back.

Ian moved his head side to side on the white pillow in a hospital bed. "Something that I can't take off, ok? That's all I'm telling you, all right?" Ian replied adamantly.

"All right, chill man," the doctor answered. Ian nodded slightly.

The doctor took some hand sanitizer and looked out the window. "They are here," he muttered.

"What?" Ian questioned behind him. "You're so dead…" "What?" Ian cried and asked again, scrambling up.

"It's it for you, little guy. You are cornered in this building…" the doctor said back. Then Ian flung himself out of the bed, pushed the curtains aside, and went to the window.

Sure enough, people (or maybe not) in green uniform marched out of a black limo. There were about eight of them that exited the vehicle.

"Don't bother leaving your room, you cannot escape!" the doctor told him. "Who are you?" Ian asked.

"A Ziknio, of course!" he told him back. "I should have known better," Ian muttered to himself as he stood up.

"Well, it was nice you accommodated me, but I need to go now, so thank you for your kindness!" Ian started walking towards the door left ajar.

The doctor stepped between him and the way out. "I am afraid you cannot leave as you wish!" the doctor said.

Ian knew he made a terrible mistake.

He should have just ran out the door. Now, Ian will need to face this guy. It wasn't going to be easy.

So Ian used the common trick.

"There is an eagle perched on the window!" Ian shouted. Ziknio fell for it. Ian took his chance to flee, and did.

"Don't run, he won't catch up to you that fast and quick," Ian uttered to himself again and again. "Just continue moving," he thought and spoke at the same time.

Ian needed to not stand out, but act as a random person in the crowds clogging the hospital corridors.

He strode calmly, while still being vigilant, with his head held high and looking at the lightbulbs, trying to avoid hospital employee's faces. Ian was still in a patient suit.

He headed for the stairways so he could go downwards towards an exit.

Ian guessed that the Zartees would use the elevator to expedite their mission to kill him instead. After all, it was a method to get out of work early.

Ian accidentally shouldered somebody as he walked by them.

Whoever was shouldered stopped behind him and lifted his hand to send a message saying that he is not too pleased. Ian ignored the sign and continued moving forward.

Then, the second incident occurred. Ian accidentally kneed a lady's purse, making her drop the purse.

Others started pointing him out to each other, muttering to their colleagues. Ian looked down at the ground, not wanting to look around as he headed straight towards the other end of the hallway.

Then his sense of hearing went to a woman talking into a phone that hung on the side of the wall. "Oh, yes, the patient hasn't been discharged, but rather gone, uh, we will bring him back immediately…"

That was it!! Ian had enough. He made long strides and went down the stairs.

Appearing on the ground level, Ian passed the pharmacy department and the café to get to the parking lot.

"Get him, anybody!" someone said from somewhere. The entire hallway that was empty suddenly became packed as doctors, nurses, and pharmacists, ran at Ian.

Ian screamed a cry of distress and ran between two people with their arms outstretched to catch him but missed.

Some employees even tried to jump on top of him and tackle Ian. Ian ducked his head many times and half-crawled through the commotion while still running.

Then Ian was charging toward the circular sliding door, which was one of those ones where you had to go in a circle to get to the other side while pushing a solid glass wall in front of you to move ahead.

Surveillance cameras attached to the corner of walls took image after image of Ian sprinting from an angry horde of employees.

At one point, he had to scoop several coins from the water fountain and throw them randomly back for distraction.

"Go, go, and go!" Ian told himself for a boost. His running form wasn't the best. It was starting to break apart.

His stomach started hurting.

Ian was sweating heavily. His arms rose and went down at a sequence, over and over again. Ian's hands were tight together, his arm curving at an acute angle.

And then, Ian's foot fell asleep. It was painful. His foot felt like it clumped together into one.

He felt like his toes didn't exist. Ian roared in pain and stumbled to keep going while yanking his leg along.

Ian would have to stop, he was tempted to. "I will not fail…" his breathless mouth said. Ian was now at half of his speed before.

Even worse, Ian went straight into a man carrying a stack of papers on one hand as he used the other to support the side of it. A rubber band kept the papers together from top to bottom. Ian collapsed on the welcome carpet.

Paper rained on everyone.

Finally, Ian's pain ceased.

He got up and went out of the hospital.

The parking lot was full of cars. Ian made sure he wasn't in the open and moved from car to car to hide.

Ian caught his breath.

Then he heard a gun shoot.

The bullet had landed on metal.

Ian put his legs behind the tire of a car next to him and lifted his head to see through the window of it.

Glass in the passenger seat on the other side fell like a chunk of ice plummeting down a glacier vertically.

Ian retreated his head.

They know where I am, he thought.

The road was damp after a storm, apparently.

Night had fallen already.

His friends must be seeking him right now.

They should be here, Ian thought.

If that was the case, he had to warn them!

But where were they?

Gunfire erupted. Glass shattered down on his head. Ian closed his eyes.

Ian noticed that he was bleeding in the left ear after touching it to check. He needed to relocate.

Then Ian went out into the open, and there, a race car was driven at him.

He had only seconds to act.

It almost hit his legs. The heat of the engine can be marked as 'very warm.'

Ian jumped on the hood of the car and held onto the windshield wipers.

The car went straight forward, towards a concrete wall. Ian let go and pushed his body to the top where he held onto the rims of the roof of the car.

The car drove in circles to try to fling Ian off, while he yelled meaningless words. Ian didn't know how he even pronounced them.

Then the sun-window was opened automatically.

A gun pointed out of it and Ian had to let go of one hand to move his body to the side so the bullets wouldn't hit him.

Then the car stopped, Ian didn't know why. Everything was calm. It was awkward and very, very weird.

"You are saved by us, dude," Drake walked out of the shadows. Everybody else followed him. "How did you guys know?" Ian asked in disbelief. "We kind of tail-backed the police cars and arrived to see you…" Joe explained.

"It was a surprise," Reeve pointed out. "You were awesome!" Jarret commented.

"Thanks," Ian said. "But we have to go now, seriously, into a different region that is not governed by this city." "Um, how are we actually going to leave this place?" Alexis questioned. Flix responded, "Don't worry, I will tell you guys the answer…"

"First step, jack a car, anyone of them," Flix told them as they got to the streets. "I will do it," Ian raised his hand.

A taxi car pulled up and halted. The guy rode down his window.

"To where?" he asked gruffly. "Nowhere, give me this," Ian cried.

Flix nudged everybody else to act tough and they quickly got into position.

The taxi man arched an eyebrow. "Listen, you and I already know the answer is NO..." "Oh man," Ian muttered to himself. "I will never be doing this again, this is the only time," Ian spoke to himself, sighing.

He broke the window, reached in to press the button that had an illustration of unlocking, and opened it.

Ian without second thought, took the guy by the collar and dragged him out of the driver's seat onto the sidewalk.

"Get in, Joe, drive like last time!" Ian said controllably.

Joe started the engine and the car started moving, gaining speed.

"Flix! Directions!" Flix moved into the passenger seat and pointed to many directions, and which route to take.

Before they knew it, green sedans followed them from behind. "There, that hole in the ground!" Flix cried. Joe swerved into the underground.

"Where are we?" "Keep going, don't ask!" Flix seemed annoyed.

They appeared in this glass tunnel. "Whoa, this is like snorkeling!" Jarret pointed out. Whales and sharks and schools of fish were visible since they were underwater now. "A glass underwater tunnel? I never heard of that! This is amazing!" Alexis exclaimed.

There was an identical one on the other side which was the way to go back. Both of the tunnels had two lanes.

A sign read: Miles-Long Tunnel, started construction in 2008, the year payed tribute to the lieutenants' deaths.

"Is this literally miles-long?" Ian asked. No one answered. "Ok, yes," he concluded since nobody knew.

The lanes gave the impression that they were levitating. Ian noticed that neon rings, with a color pattern, extended from beneath to the ceiling. The colors were like *dancing*.

This was one bright tunnel in the ocean.

Then Drake noticed something. "There's a helicopter equipped with machine guns coming from the right side!"

And yet, "Joe, go faster, or we will be shot into the ocean, come on!" Reeve cried. It was clear that the helicopter was targeting them.

Its guns followed them.

The glass behind was vanishing.

Cars fell into the sea. Large species gobbled them up. Tons of water blasted into the tunnel and was rapidly accumulating as it headed towards them.

There was just too much to process that Ian completely doze off somehow.

After what was like half an hour, Ian awoke to a complaint. "We are almost out of gas!" Joe screamed.

"Hang on, we can get there," Flix told them. The car went several more feet, lurched and went into the underground again, appearing in broad daylight on a patch of grass. There, the car broke down. Airbags shot out.

"It's funny how you guys were wowed by the features, and then suddenly apprehensive to get back on land," Joe said. "This should be an awesome day to remember in the future, if when anytime we have to tell this story," Joe added, chuckling.

Chapter Eleven: The Basic Lifestyle

They now had to continue on foot. Ian saw that up ahead was a town with low-standing buildings that were approximately 5 feet high and 5 feet wide.

They were all the same. The town gradually extended upwards onto a hill and beyond. But there weren't any roads, just grass. It was like a ghost town in the countryside.

"Is there another route around this spooky place to get back to where we belong?" Drake asked Joe. He shrugged and said, "I really don't know," and, "Tell Flix that!" Drake then went to question him.

A poster on a piece of cardboard hanging on a single nail with a piece of string read: Once an affluent area, but not anymore (and) population— 10. When Ian spotted the number, he was not too comfortable with the fact of that. They barely noticed a man behind it holding the sign up as if he was a block of steel.

Joe hopped backwards, putting a hand to his heart. The man was grinning.

"Well, how are you friends' doin'?" the person waved a wrinkled and fat hand looking like it was inflated with air.

He was wearing a hat made of hay and had little teeth inside his mouth when he smiled an exaggerated one.

Blotches of dirt (dried) was on the guy's cheeks.

His hair was uneven and his face was almost as round as a watermelon. The man was very skinny and had a stiff neck.

He was like in his 20s or 30s.

"This person is totally drawn away from the rest of society and urban life. He does not act the same or even dress the same, like formally or casually," Alexis whispered to Joe.

"Does he even shower or take a bath?" Jarret thought to Drake.

"I said, what up? I am described as Jaden!" "Isn't it 'my name is Jaden' instead?" Drake talked back.

Alexis nudged him to keep quiet.

Ian thought she thought he was condescending Jaden, who just had a different style of language.

"Yes, if you suppose, I am now the guide of your tour!" Jaden replied.

Drake was going to say something but then both Reeve and Joe covered his face and Ian could only hear him grumble a word.

Jaden didn't even flinch or look at them, but turned around. "With me we proceed!" he mumbled.

Jarret went in the front, Flix behind him. Joe third, and Ian fourth.

Their stop was a control tower looking thing like one of those at the airport, except it was 50 times shorter.

A half-oval shaped door slid into the side to reveal a path for them. Ian entered and immediately looked up to see sunlight flash in from the very top.

"The stairs! Go move up!" Each set of them kept tracing to the other one. For example, you would have to walk up one flight then turn left to do the same thing again. They had to repeat the procedure a few times.

It was very dangerous because there were not any railings to make sure if you topple sideways, you wouldn't at least fall onto the pavement below and die!

They kept going and moving.

Joe came into this viewing area that was only like 15 feet off the ground. "Wow, I can *totally* see everything up here!" "Yup, absolutely!" Jarret agreed.

Jaden didn't realize what they said, or probably didn't care.

"Here, see people? Watch and study and observe actions they make!" Jaden told them. Ian focused on this particular girl.

She was very attractive with curly hair that covered the sides and her head behind. It dropped down to her shoulders, resting on it. The girl had an indistinguishable color of skin between light coffee and white chocolate. She wore a very dazzling and eye-catching dress with many of the rainbow colors.

It was very flamboyant. Almost everything was perfect about her. The eyelashes were the right amount that extended upwards, catching little pieces of the air. Her skin was very clean and shone in the light of day.

But something about her was peculiar. Ian was already looking at her for about a minute. She kept walking the same places, streets, and roads she had just a minute ago. The girl also didn't have a smile on her mouth.

Ian wasn't about to tell his friends what he suspected, but then... "Guys, come over here! I found something out!" Drake's mouth burst open, apparently he was let go, which wasn't a very wise thing.

"Look! Watch that lady!" She kept strolling in circles around a 30 feet diameter. "Me too!" Joe came *crashing* in.

FYI, Drake always fell for girls older than him, all the time.

"What is going on?" Alexis cried. Reeve seemed lost and confused.

Flix kept quiet, somehow.

Jaden sensed that something was wrong too. "So, the matt'r, wha' ees eet?" "What is the meaning of this?" Joe tried to look tough and walked up to Jaden.

"What kind of witchcraft and magic is this?" Alexis yelled.

"Tell us or you will pay for this!" Reeve shouted.

"End! No panic! Let I explain!" Jaden responded.

"Go ahead! Let me see if you are lying or telling the truth!" Joe said back.

Jaden cleared his throat. Ian knew he drank and ate much dairy because of the mucus in his throat.

"We are born, followin' a way of life, and a system of daily life," Jaden spoke slowly. "I don't get it, I don't speak your language!" Drake pointed at him offensively.

Jaden seemed sad.

"Our town, or maybe even city…Fayse, lacks entertainment and enjoyment of life. Life is not supposed to be fun for us, and is pretty boring, but we are taught to have fun despite this…" Jaden suddenly halted, and then concluded, "Yes, yeah, thank you for listening."

"You said 'we are taught' so who taught you guys?" Joe questioned.

Jaden hesitated.

Jaden dropped to his knees and put his hands together.

"Please! I'm begging you, I can't say!" Jaden cried, tears streaming down his cheeks. Ian realized they cleaned up his face because of the dirt.

Then Joe attempted to force it out of him. He brandished his staff. The crystal was put on the top while they were on the ship that sank. It shone with dignity.

Joe put it across his neck. "One touch of this, and you are dead!" he said calmly into Jaden's ear.

Jaden whimpered.

"Fine, here you go. There is a man who sits on top of the hill up there, you see it? He is an elder and an old man. He bears the answer to this mystery. But I warn you guys, don't touch his nerves or he will…!"

"Excellent, let's go!" Joe started down the stairs. "See you later, Jaden!" Joe teased on his way down. The rest of them followed reluctantly and with loath.

✳ ✳ ✳

The old man was sitting in hero-position. He had a very whitish-gray long beard that dropped all the way to the ground.

He sat between two trees. "I don't think he ever shaved," Drake whispered.

"What?!" the man shouted, his eyes opening from meditating.

"Don't try to bad-talk me, because it won't work!" he screamed.

Then, ninjas were somehow appearing in thin air, getting summoned.

This was bad.

"Attack! Charge!" Joe cried.

Joe charged his staff like it was a spear at a ninja who wasn't looking at him until realizing, which was too late. The ninja was driven into a tree, his belly pinned.

Alexis stood there to think of something, like she was lost in thought, daydreaming. "Alexis!" Ian hurried towards her.

Then, after two seconds, several deer galloped and halted next to Alexis, as if they were doing a salute. Others galloped from the dense forest.

The skirmish began.

Then Ian realized his team was losing. Help, he thought over and over again.

Then Jaden appeared. "Hey! I was actually hired to do this!"

Ian stopped what he was doing. Jaden was staring at him in particular.

"I am sorry, I pretended to speak different English because I was required to by taking up this job."

"You have broken the rules! Now you must die and perish!" the old man cried. "Does he even have a name?" Drake asked.

Joe stepped between the old man and Jaden. "You will have to get through me before…" "Oh, I will!" the old man had his own staff appear in his clutched hand.

They clashed.

Their swords resembled an "x" while constraining on each other. Jaden looked like he didn't know what he should be doing right at that spot. He seemed lost. Ian tried to signal him to help Joe.

"Stop!" the atmosphere suddenly turned dark. Daylight disappeared. Mist swirled around all of them. An oval-shaped space appeared in the center of a cloud of mist.

"I can barely see!" Jarret cried. "What is this?" the old man questioned into the environment.

"There is no need to know, weakling!" the Mist shouted back. "How dare…" the old man was thrown into the air and slammed back into the ground. He immediately fainted and lost consciousness. Or maybe he was dead.

"Ian!" Ian shook from left to right several times, his eyes widening. "Remember me? At your home's doorstep with that sickening sword?" Ian went blank for a moment before recalling the time he lost his father.

Ian fought back tears. He wasn't going to embarrass himself in front of his friends and possibly strangers watching.

"Go ahead! I profoundly understand your pain! Cry like it doesn't matter anymore! Sob like you are at home!" the Haunter spoke, the oval-shaped blanket of air (which was his mouth) moving and twitching.

"No! I won't!" Ian threw himself at the Mist. But it left and became visible next to him like it teleported. Tears rolled down Ian's cheeks. But they weren't tears of despondence, but rather tears of rage.

"You will not leave without paying a price! Be punished!" Ian yelled without second thought or consideration.

116

His statement was far from true. Ian believed in miracles, but they somehow always happened at the most not-needed times. But when Ian needed them most, they didn't occur all the time.

He wished he had a power to create miracles when he wanted to because right now was a good time.

"Here, what about this? I will never arrive and annoy you ever again if you would stay put in this town for the rest of your life? Think of it, no more harm coming your way!" the Haunter asked convincingly.

Ian thought of this. He couldn't just watch the world fall to The Haunter. When he takes over the world, everybody including people I know and me are doomed, he thought. Life will be much harder and even worse.

"Denied!" Ian concluded.

"Oh! Wow! I have been turned down! Well, too bad for you…" The Haunter started but didn't continue. Then, The Haunter assembled an arm out of the mist. There was no hand at the end of it. "I will take a prisoner from here on!" The Haunter jabbed his arm and it went within a foot of Jaden's abdomen. He was lifted.

Jaden's head dropped back as he was leveled into midair.

Joe lunged at The Haunter and lifted his staff, the crystal pointing at the Mist. One quick stab, and Ian heard the Haunter wail a very agonizing noise.

The Mist swirled in a funnel into the sky and daylight bloomed. Jaden was gone along with The Haunter.

"Why did you do that? He was holding someone hostage we knew!" Alexis screamed at Joe.

"Don't tell me you like him…" Reeve grinned evilly. "You're crazy!" Alexis looked away, her face a tad flustered. "Joe! Answer me!" "We barely knew him, all right?" Joe replied. "Well, you could have been a gentleman and helped him, by that I mean save his life! He's a living soul too like each one of us!" Alexis said back.

"Girl, Joe's right, it's okay," Drake came over and substantiated. "Yeah, he's telling the right thing," Reeve agreed.

Alexis took a few minutes to calm down and was herself again.

Chapter Twelve: The Four Steps

Joe stepped on something hard. He lifted his foot and reached his hand forward, picking up a badge resembling the shape of a heart but not exactly.

Ian gathered with everyone else around Joe as he settled the copper item on his palm. "What is that?" Reeve asked.

"I don't know, there are words engraved on the surface, in the middle," Joe muttered back, not taking his eyes off the object like it was gold he had found himself.

"I can't read off of it, it is too dark now, plus I am getting very hungry!" Jarret complained. Blake, who had been on Flix's shoulder was yawning constantly and rubbing his tummy a lot. "Let's just settle for the night," Joe suggested. They agreed without reluctance.

"Um, uh, where are our duffel bags?" Drake suddenly looked alert. "Oh, there, I thought…" "Please don't talk," Reeve put a hand up into the air which made him go hush.

"We've run out of food!" Drake cried after looking into the bags. "No way! I don't believe it!" he yelled.

"Also, our things are gone! Only our tents are here!" Drake yelled again. "I think we dropped and lost much of it especially when we were about to die…" Alexis pointed out.

So they set-up their tents under the two trees across from each other.

As night fell, Ian couldn't sleep in his personal tent. There was just too much going on in his mind. His brain was clogged.

Ian decided to go outside for a walk. The scenery was amazing. Nature was beautiful especially at night.

Ian sat and then realized there were footsteps behind him. Somebody touched his shoulder gently. It was Alexis who sat down next to him on the soft grass.

"Pretty, right?" "Yeah," Ian answered, his tone changing a bit.

"I used to always sneak outdoors to watch nature and be in the environment. I don't remember my past before moving to Yart. When I met you, I knew you were a good person and a potential friend, you know, that sort of thing. My parents had abandoned me for sure. Then, I was picked-up by an old granny," Alexis said like a storyteller.

Ian didn't say anything and didn't know why she was telling him her personal stuff. "I was taken into a warm house with cookies every meal I could chew on. The granny loved me. One night, she told me how she had lost a loved one too, her own daughter."

"Before Joe told her I was going on a quest to 'save the world' she was a bit confused and couldn't let me go. Joe had personally went to my house to try to get me to go on the quest. But of course, he had to get through my granny. She didn't let me go easily."

"My granny negotiated over and over again while I sat on the couch listening to the conversation. Part of it was in my own room. Finally, she let me go and agreed. It was painful for her. She told me that 'be careful and always remember me.' My granny said I was a nice girl and every time I wake up, I remember her voice and the same phrase."

Alexis smiled a sad one.

"I wished she was here…" Alexis said, burying her head in her arm. Without thinking, Ian wrapped an arm around her. It was like stimuli and response. It was automatic. What else could he do? Watch her? Alexis was homesick.

"Thank you, I am deeply grateful for you, you are like my granny who has always kept me safe and comforted," Alexis smiled a happier smile, and that surely made and triggered Ian's insides to jump.

She immediately got up and walked back to her tent and went in.

Ian was so tired that he fell asleep right there.

Morning arrived and Ian wasn't up yet. Joe had to *wrench* him awake. "Why are you out here, son? Enjoying the view all night?" Joe asked suspiciously.

Joe took out the badge he found last night and read, "I am a terrorist from Dop, a city to which our central base is, dot, dot." "What kind of joke is this?" Joe thought.

"Hey Joe! You know what day of the week it is? I have lost track!" Jarret asked. "Never mind that, I have to get this back to Kakutah!" Flix stood there and shook his head.

"Why not?" Joe asked. "Kakutah is under lockdown and inspection of the ruckus we caused..." Flix replied.

"Here, let me check." Flix vanished and appeared after two seconds or so. "Yes, I was right indeed!"

"Where's the nearest city? I need to get this to the government!" "Oh, you wouldn't want to know! Farther than the eye can see, that is all I am giving you!" Flix replied.

"Aw! Come on!" "Yup!" "We should continue to move," Joe said.

Ian observed that Joe was now almost never letting go of his staff, but carrying it around like it was a prize he wanted to show-off. Drake however kept his glade in his tent.

Jarret still didn't have a weapon, but Ian knew he was too young for one. Jarret wasn't a very responsible person.

"Flix! Why can't you just Shadow-Travel us to the city that is…I don't know, like tons of miles away?" Joe yelled. "My powers have been limited since going back to my homeland," Flix responded.

"Dang, darn," Joe uttered.

Then Ian spotted Alexis. She had gone out of her tent. The weather was nice outside. It was sunny unlike the days before.

Alexis saw Ian and just waved and smiled before joining the rest of the crowd packing up. Ian thought that she needed alone time before they could talk again.

"Let's go!" Joe shouted like he was the head coach of a sport team. Jarret groaned and dragged his belongings along.

"Flix! Can you at least Shadow-Travel back some food for us? I'm on the verge of starving," Joe cried back. "I am sorry, but my powers are only used during emergencies, not for pleasure!" Flix told him.

"But this *is* an emergency! I am about to die!" Joe said back.

"Oh, really?" Flix questioned.

"Oh well, if you will not, I would rather not keep telling you the same thing over and over again," Joe concluded.

"Wait!" Joe abruptly bounced. "I remembered you said something about how your 'powers' were limited, can you please explain?" Joe requested.

"Oh, human," Flix rolled his blue-eyes (dots). "Too many questions you ask me daily, can you bug somebody else instead?"

"There is a source of every Shadow Clan's neon electricity, and it is somewhere that I don't even know of, hidden in a place extremely covert and almost impossible to discover. What I do know is that it is not in the Shadow Clan territory but physically connects to it," Flix explained. "Here's some more."

"If you alone can break 4 steps which I will list in a moment, you are already very fortunate. The 4 steps are: break the Anything Code, get to the center of Zark, a city controlled by unknown living creatures, burn down a sacred palace, and while doing this, never forsake your friends which is one of the steps and is somehow the most important of all..." Flix pointed out.

"Wait, how do you know all this, and how can I be sure you are trustworthy?" Joe challenged. "You make the choice," Flix replied. "Um, when you said 'you are already very fortunate' what do you mean? And where do I start? What is this Zark, Anything Code, and sacred palace? Where are these *stuff* located?" Joe blurted, handing over a deluge of questions to Flix.

"Follow your instincts, do not worry!" "What? How would I know if my instincts are trustable?"

"I mean, that is clearly insane!" "Follow what your heart instructs you to do then…" "But…" "This has been my experience…" "Uh, how old are you even? And how is conquering these four steps supposed to bring me closer to getting to the source of…whatever?" "It will tell you the answer, by the way. Ok, listen, I have been banished from my own homeland, I'm trying to recover, and my friends have let me down, so please leave me alone! All right? I will tell you more another day," Flix said. "Chill! So emotional! Fine! I will ignore you for the rest of the trip!" Joe looked away.

Joe was very confused and expected more information. But Flix disappeared in the shadows to somewhere safe and sound to be in peace, Ian hoped.

Ian overhead all this. He sensed that things were getting more serious.

Ian went to sit under the shade for a while. He looked at his Wrist Striker which he was used to wearing already. It felt like a part of his arm. Ian saw that there was much dirt spattered on it. "Oh, man," he muttered.

Ian got up and started punching the air around him, practicing.

126

Ian thought that he needed to train his close combat skills. And then he saw someone doing about the same thing as him.

Joe.

He had his teeth clenched and doing pushups, jumping jacks, and many other different warm up exercises before standing up and starting to use his hands and feet to attack the air around him. Ian wondered why he was doing that. "Joe! What are you doing?" Joe twisted his head to look at him.

"Oh! Just trying to get buffer because it is my job to do so. Couple days ago, I just realized. I am the chaperone, right, and I am supposed to be like the bodyguard and protect everybody else here including you!"

Ian walked away, thinking about it like it deserved a 'w-o-w.'

Joe was a partly-changed man. Was he really doing it for them? Why was he willing to take-up this task to work for them? These were questions lingering in Ian's head. Joe was working hard, very hard. Then a topic went to mind. "Hey Joe! I remember from weeks ago that you were something called a Gock?" Joe stopped suddenly in his moves.

"Do not say that ever again, not even in your mind, I do not like to talk about that!" Joe warned. He continued his training like he was in a military school and camp.

Ian knew he had touched a nerve because of how Joe didn't use the possible contractions don't instead of do not.

Finally, they all packed-up their tents and possibly weapons.

With that, they continued the trek.

Chapter Thirteen: The Simulation

Not everyone cooperated during the long walk of about an hour. Finally they halted at this stream only two feet wide and nine feet in length. On the other side was an area of many *lumps* of light-colored sand.

"Um, this place is weird. I have never seen such a landscape before. What the heck is this? Is that bluish-white sand? It sure looks like a desert of some kind, but how would one be so up in the North?" Reeve thought.

"Another desert? Are you seriously kidding me?" Jarret asked. "Well, what other option to we have? Let's keep going!" Drake suggested. The others didn't move until Joe nodded approval reluctantly.

The sand was very slushy. Ian went to Drake's side and elbowed him. Lately, they haven't been talking much. Ian wanted to, but somehow feared the fact of that. They used to have many topics to chat about.

After a long time, Ian looked back and couldn't see where they came from anymore. Then this was when the ground shook. A hole opened up in the middle of a lump. Ian nearly fell into it but was caught by Joe.

The lumps started going back and forth all over the terrain like it were waves in the sea, rolling all over the place. Ian and his friends were scattered.

"Welcome to the dunes, the Cold Dunes!" Ian recognized the voice.

He looked up into the distance.

Lady Harsh was floating through the air towards them in a crisscross-applesauce sitting form.

"Under these dunes are spikes you might fall on, so get ready!"

Ian glanced at his Wrist Striker. He was going to defend himself.

But one thing prevented him from doing so. His hand was stuck in the sand on top of a lump. Ian struggled to get it out as Lady Harsh was floating slowly at them. She was indeed doing some magic. Then, she raised her hand elegantly. Ian feared the worse and closed his eyes. The terrain started moving around once again. Ian was about to puke.

Somehow, a blast of heat that looked like a miniature comet flew from his Wrist Striker and shot into the distance.

Ian didn't know what happened. Did his gadget malfunction? He was as surprised as the others around him.

Then, after checking his gadget for a moment, he found out. There was a piece of thin wire with rubber wrapped around it. He was grasping it before the blast occurred and let go. Just squeeze it to shoot, Ian considered. He tried again, and it worked.

But he lost concentration while tumbling and rolling around in the sand. Ian was reminded of how he used to go to the beach and get sand all over him.

"You, Ian, will be the one to die before anybody else!" Lady Harsh screamed, getting closer to him.

Ian spotted a boulder, half of it submerged in the sand. I need to get there! He thought. Ian headed that way.

Then Lady Harsh started throwing her signature ninja stars. Ian dodged a couple and took his hand to slap it on the top of the rock, his palm face-down.

Ian slid up and got up. He took a look at his gadget. "Let's do this!"

Ian shot several comets out of his Wrist Striker. He'd aimed at Lady Harsh. The ammo went straight through her. Holes appeared in Lady Harsh' coat.

Lady Harsh fell back through the air. Ian thought he killed her. He was about to roar in triumph.

But then, Lady Harsh stood back up in the air and charged (flew quickly) straight at Ian and the rock he was standing upon. Ian was so afraid that he fell backwards onto the sand and started sinking in.

No, he thought. The sand was engulfing him. Ian tried to sit up but couldn't. Attempt after attempt, the sand stuck onto him from every angle. Lady Harsh stood over him on the boulder before he knew it.

She smiled maliciously. Her hands became Fists and she put them together (touching by knuckle) just above her chest. Then, with a yell, her hand went apart, Fingers flying individually. The rock broke in half.

Drake came behind Lady Harsh and swiped at her back with his glade.

Lady Harsh stuttered, her eyes deadlock, her mouth opened slightly.

She started shimmering and became blurry. "You haven't seen the last of me yet!" and Lady Harsh vanished.

Afterwards, Drake was highly honored and congratulated. Usually, he would go with his friends to an ice cream shop but it turned out not the case for this place. I mean, where would one be found in the wilderness?

The dunes seemed as though they were chunks of ice and melted, revealing grassland underneath.

Chapter Fourteen: The Frantic Search

"Dang, I need a pit-stop," Drake pointed out.
"Yeah," Jarret agreed.

Lately, Drake had become good friends with Jarret instead of continuing his own friendship with Ian.

Ian felt different without a buddy to talk too constantly. Every time Ian tried to stir up a conversation, Drake reacted by ignoring. Now, since meeting Jarret, Drake had found a potential friend. Ian was not sure why Drake didn't speak a word with him anymore.

So, Ian decided to walk over to Joe and start exchanging some words with him. He made sure his back was to Drake to make him jealous. "Hey!" Ian said.

Joe barely looked sideways at him. "What? I am thinking right now, don't disturb me! It is called alone time, and severe contemplation!" Joe pointed out.

"Oh, oh, okay, keep going…" Ian faced the landscape again, strolling alongside Joe. He hoped Drake was watching while he was giggling with Jarret behind him.

What were they laughing about? Ian suspected that they were pointing at and making fun of him.

"You know," Joe elbowed Ian, "Do you actually think Flix is loyal to us? I mean, I kind of doubt it because he always leaves us and uses his *magic* to fly away invisibly or something to somewhere we don't know. What if he is doing something bad behind our backs? Is Flix trying to play a game with us by pretending to help us?" Joe raised. Ian considered this.

Joe had used to be a janitor and a very humorous guy. Who knew he would raise a question like this about one who has protected them so much?

"Joe, Flix has saved us many times by now, you really think he is trying to hurt us?" Ian inquired.

"Possibly," Joe answered. "I don't know," Joe added.

Then there was silence in the team. Ian risked a glance back and saw that Drake and Joe were walking like zombies. Ian knew they were exhausted.

The energy was gone.

"How long?" Reeve questioned nature. "Patience!" Joe said back.

"Are we even going the right way? Do you have a compass?" Reeve asked. Joe took one out of his sleeve.

"Yup! Moving north!" "It's getting cold! I need a jacket. My kind cannot defend themselves from cold air!" Reeve told him, for she lived her whole life near the tropic.

"Do you have a thermometer too?" Reeve asked. "Uh, I think so…" and after rummaging in all the pockets he had in his clothing, said, "No, it's not even important!"

"Yo! I see a person riding some…mule or pony? And also dragging…? You know what? I can't tell, but he is coming towards us, get prepared, be ready, we have company!" Drake piped.

"Stand aside! Your eyesight isn't even legit! Let the master see!" Joe took his hand and shoved Drake's arm away from him. "You…!" Joe looked into the open space.

The orange sunset made it hard to look into the distance. "Oh, here he comes, let's see if he would give us a ride! And what is he doing here? He looks like a merchant!"

136

"I mean, what kind of *alien* is this?" Joe complained.

"There, there, who knows what? He might and may be a nice person who wants to help us strangers! Ever heard of the Good Samaritan, eh? Answer me!" said Alexis, who was always on the bright side.

The man came closer and closer. "Hey! Who are you?" Drake shouted out. The man stared blankly at him, unblinking. They were dark colored, very abnormal. He wore a green cloth over his head. His face was serious. His mouth unmoving for a moment.

"Hey! Can we borrow your little horses for a ride north, just to the nearest city?" Joe asked the person.

Then, a smooth and monotone voice spoke, "Yes, you surely may!" The man's face was expressionless.

Joe took a step forward and immediately, the mysterious man held up a hand. "Wait! I choose and pick for you!"

Joe lifted his head. The man pointed to a specific mule and did the same for the others including Ian.

"You sure about this?" Reeve and Jarret asked Joe at the same time. Joe put his head down and said, "Yeah! I guess so."

"Um, do you know how to ride one of these?" Drake asked anyone. "Learn!" Ian answered.

"One more thing," the guy spoke. "Let me touch that crystal!"

Joe had it cuddled in his arms even though it was very heavy. After all, it was a prized possession.

Suddenly, the purple air inside the crystal started moving in circles. A dragon's head appeared like it was trying to escape. Ian recognized it.

"Hot, hot, hot, ouch!" Joe cried. "Lend me the crystal," the man said afterwards, and you will not have to go through this! Joe fell for it. He gave it to the man.

"Well, thank you, here's a last gift!" the man tossed a brass circular item connected to a bronze chain to Joe who was recovering and rubbing his hands with his sleeves. Ian caught whatever it was. It sat neatly in his palm.

They mounted their mules.

"What the," Ian yelled. The man gave out his true identity.

It wrote:

I am a bandit, similar to those wandering the wilderness. Thank you for this valuable possession.

The horses I have so kindly offered to you are crazy ones. They will do whatever to fling you off, drive into a tree, or anything perilous enough to certainly kill you. Do not underestimate the horses. They will put you on the Highway to Hell.

Having the crystal neatly between his arm and body, he took off on his own horse. "After him! He is a thief and deceiver!" Ian shouted and cried.

Jarret thought he knew everything about being a horseman by taking the strap and slapping it on his horse's neck. The horse whinnied, lifting its two legs off the ground and Jarret fell onto the ground.

Ian extended his hand to Jarret and he took it. Ian pulled him onto his own horse behind him. "Are you sure it can withstand both of us?" Jarret asked. "I'm not sure," Ian said honestly. "Probably not!" Ian added.

"Follow the bandit!" Joe yelled.

The horses ran after the man. Joe's ran in a straight line. But the others ran sideways, diagonal, and anything but straight.

Reeve's horse refused to move and hampered around in circles, kicking dust into the air. Reeve cursed.

Alexis' horse went to the other way and she struggled to pull back the reins. She somehow was indeed successful.

The bandit was almost out of sight, but they managed to catch-up to 15 feet of him. The bandit, with his skills, took out a revolver from his belt. He looked back.

Spinning the revolver, the bandit shot at Joe and missed. Joe cocked his head to the side to let the bullet pass.

It went on for a while, or shall I say a pretty long time.

Finally, the bandit was careless without looking forward and his horse ran off the cliff ahead. He fell with his horse. Joe halted his. Ian halted his.

"The crystal!" Alexis cried. "Oh no!" Joe seemed indifferent. "Don't worry, it fell into the bay over there, we can go retrieve it tomorrow after a good rest!" "How?" Reeve asked. "By going underwater, duh!" Joe said like it was obvious. "Do you have a brain? Or are you a no brainer?"

A small town with skyscrapers sat on the beach. "I can spot a scuba-diving store over there, you see that sign? This will be easy!" Joe pointed out. "Joe! Are you in your right mind?" Alexis questioned.

"It might be gone forever, you know!" Reeve retorted.

"Hey guys! That bandit died painfully!" Drake interrupted. "Yeah! That was so awesome!" Jarret agreed. Ian wanted to join in but somehow couldn't. His dignity didn't allow him to and he didn't know why. If you did in fact join in, he would betray his dignity.

So they camped right at that spot for the cold night.

141

Ian watched the sunrise. At last, everybody was up. The ocean water glimmered and glittered. There was a boardwalk. They had to hike down the mountain to get there.

"I used to love being next to the beach, with all those shops, and the breezy air!" Alexis said charmingly. "Are you kidding me? It is horrible here, too developed, metropolitan, not my style!" Reeve didn't agree. Alexis crossed her arms. She didn't respond or reply.

"But you can't say you don't like shopping, right?" Alexis asked Reeve. "Um…nope! I actually do not like to shop! I come from a place where what you absolutely need is provided already."

"But what about things who want?" Alexis asked. "In my homeland, we learn how to use what there is rather than desiring for stuff unnecessary," Reeve answered. Alexis didn't see the point in continuing to argue.

"We have got to warn the people here about the threat of Shadow Clan!" Alexis said rather. "Let us complete one project before going on to the next one, okay? That is searching for the crystal!" Joe replied.

Alexis snorted.

142

"Also, if we do warn them, we will be an obvious group of people, and the Press will track us, raising suspicion. That will be the last scenario we need to encounter and be in," Joe reported to Alexis particularly and especially. "Yeah, he is right," Drake agreed.

"I love this place! I want to stay and live here forever! At night, it must be very glamorous and bright!" Jarret announced.

"I love the costal feel!" Jarret said. "But why is the water murky?" "Pollution," Joe responded.

"Joe! Can we stay here for a bit?" Alexis asked hopefully. "Well, uh, but we have to go home…actually, I guess so!" Joe said. Ian could see excitement on his face.

"Ouch! Ow….!" Drake exclaimed. "What happened?" Ian reacted. As he lifted up his foot, Ian saw a piece of a clam shell attached to the bottom. "Careful! Shattered shells are all over the beach!" Ian taught him.

"Drake! Why did you take of your shoes?" Alexis questioned with an attitude that suggested he was nasty. "The sand is very soft! It feels comfortable! I like it!"

"All right, everybody together, huddle up!" Joe beckoned. "But it would be awkward!" Ian blurted. Joe ignored him.

"Meet me back here in two hours. Now, go have fun!" Joe dismissed.

"Can I come with you?" Ian asked.

"Why?" Joe questioned thoughtfully. "Because I want to be with you instead..." Ian replied simply. "What about your friends? Was there a disagreement?" Joe asked. "No, no, it's just I don't want to leave you alone," Ian responded casually.

"Fine, come, we are going to the Snorkel Store," Joe beckoned.

Ian looked back and saw that Alexis, Drake, Reeve, and Jarret were heading to a store called Sun-Blocks and Sandal Fashion. Joe eyed him wearily like he was trying to read Ian off his expression.

"Uh, Joe? How are we going to see in the murky water? I mean, it is a color between black and brown!" Ian asked.

"That is why I brought a water-filter that is the size of one and a half of my hands!" Joe replied. Ian chuckled. "Yeah, those hands are quite big!"

They entered the store and immediately, snorkel gear appeared on each rack. The goggles had plastic tubes that went up for the availability to breath air. Hermit crabs were for sale for only 5 bucks including the tanks. A salesman came up to them and assisted them.

"So, what can I do for you, gentlemen?" "Oh, do you sell scuba-diving suits here?" Joe asked. "Yes, in the back, here, please wait for a moment, I'm going to get it," the salesman turned around and went to the back. After about four minutes, he walked back.

"Here you go," the salesman gave the purple, dark blue, and black suit to Joe. "And what's the price?" Ian asked. "30 dollars at the cashier!"

"Joe, that is quite pricey, don't you think so?" Ian glanced at him. Joe didn't waste any time or even look back at him. He concluded, "I am going to take it, besides, it is not too much!" Ian was amazed.

Joe walked indifferently to the cashier and payed with cash. The salesman took it happily and gave him the suit.

"Do you know where I can dive?" Joe asked. "Oh, um, there is an extension into the water of the boardwalk just a half a mile from here. Take a right, it is next to the Ferris Wheel, thank you for shopping here and with us, we hope you come back soon," the salesman responded, and went on to assist another.

"Hey! What about me?" Ian asked.

"What do you mean?" Joe inquired. "I'm going in with you! I need a suit too!" Ian answered.

"That's silly. You have a more important task," Joe replied to him. "And what is that task?" Ian asked him.

"Oh, making sure I don't sink or drown. Pretty sure making sure I don't die by saving me if I have trouble somehow," Joe said.

"How?" Ian wondered. "Oh! With that G-hook of yours, of course!"

As they walked the boardwalk, their feet hit the wood, making a *clock clock* sound. The strips of wood were organized and glued together diagonally.

Finally the extension came into sight. "There we go!" Joe exclaimed. "Yay! We are here!" Ian agreed.

"Not yet! Just a few more steps!" Joe pointed out.

Then they really got there.

"All right, you stay up here," Joe said before putting on his goggles and flippers. "If I say 'help' throw that hook to me and pull me back!" Joe wagged a Finger.

Ian knew he was a tad afraid because he was shaking from head to foot like he was freezing outside in the winter.

✳ ✳ ✳

Joe rubbed his shoulder blades and eyes. He ruffled his hair.

"Goodbye for now, keep a good eye on me!" Joe said to Ian.

Joe glanced at the scenery and then the dark blue water which was supposed to be white. But the sun didn't allow it.

Before Ian could reply, Joe dove into the cold water below.

At the beginning, Joe couldn't see at all. He felt water pressure as he went down. No, this can't be, Joe thought.

Then, Joe tried moving around and was successful. He took out his filter and blasted all the dirty stuff into itself. Light blue and red coral came into view all over the bay floor.

Where could it be? Joe thought.

He kept floating around and suddenly became very lost. Stay in this area, Joe thought to himself.

The crystal could be anywhere. Joe feared the worst.

Which way should I go? He thought.

Joe hobbled around in the water for a while. He lost track of time.

Joe was going to count second by second to get a good sense of timing but lost count right after crashing into the cold water. How long has it been? Joe became very panicky and impatient.

He wasn't comfortable underwater in an artic reef. Just get the crystal and it will be all over, Joe thought.

After what seemed like forever, Joe thought, how much time has passed? He wanted to get out desperately. Why didn't I get a waterproof watch? Joe thought.

He regret not having one.

Joe started dividing different areas into sections where he thought the crystal fell. One by one, he looked over and studied the ocean ground. No crystal.

Has it been two hours already? Joe thought. It must have been, he assumed with reluctance. Joe wasn't sure.

Then there was a sparkle of purple. Joe caught it with the corner of his eye. But after what seemed less than a second, it was gone already and didn't flash again.

He bobbled around until getting to a clearing. Sunlight penetrated the surface, making it not impervious.

Bluish colonies of fish swam together around pieces of coral while 5-10 feet sharks in length circled them. Starfish sat sprawled on the ocean floor. Seaweed and kelp rose from the bottom.

What now? Joe thought.

Then, he spotted the object. It had a purple glimmer to it, but Joe wasn't sure if it was in fact the crystal. I will have to get closer, Joe thought to himself.

Joe floated towards the unknown object. That was when a muscular creature with fins appeared right on front of his body. It took him several seconds to piece the situation together. Blacktip, whitetip, and grey reef sharks circled the object, surrounding it like it was worth guarding. Oh no, Joe thought.

Come on, leave! Joe gritted his teeth and said to his own mind. This is going to be impossible.

No way, I'm not heading through those wall of sharks!

I will surely get eaten alive before I even know what is going on! Joe thought. He knew this was going to be hard, at least for him.

I volunteered to be the chaperone, Joe thought to himself. I will be the tough guy, not the coward!

Joe dodged the sharks and entered. His hand cuddled around the crystal and he slid it up to his armpit. Joe was sweating, partly because he was hot in the suit, but most of it was because he was extremely nervous.

He would never be able to describe the fear and anxiety. Joe knew it almost immediately as he saw the black dots staring at him. They were the sharks' eyes.

$$*\,*\,*$$

Ian saw Joe dive into the bay and he lost sight of him. He worried about him and hoped he was okay.

Ian sat on the boardwalk extension while watching kids play in the sand and splashing water at each other.

Time went by fast. Ian wondered how long Joe would take.

Ian fell asleep a few times during his watch. Finally, he thought he saw a human hand go up out of the water.

Ian missed it and waited for it to come out again for confirmation.

After an entire minute that felt oddly long, it poked out of the water. Ian saw that ripples were being made from where the hand was. There must be some action under there.

Ian pressed the red button on his Wrist Striker, and a metal claw-like thing shot out of an opening in the front of it. Ian moved his hand around to get the g-hook to where he wanted it to land.

It splashed the water and the hand tried desperately to get a hold of it. Then, Ian felt something tugging on it. He saw something of a gray top and a white underside. Ian was flung into the water in no time.

The sudden feeling of freezing water didn't suit Ian's warm-blooded body. It stung in a way. Ian screamed.

Ian wasn't always a good swimmer. He tried doing free-style the other way, but the shark was dragging him backwards.

Ian wanted to cry like a baby. His life was about to end quickly and abruptly. At least he didn't need to suffer that much. How much would it hurt?

Then, the dragging stopped. Ian risked a glimpse back.

The human hand and arm was wrestling with the shark.

Ian swam to the shore.

Joe's head appeared, his mouth opening and closing. He was gasping for air. Joe took hold of the hook.

Ian pressed the 'reverse' button and the hook retracted. Joe shot out of the bay and the shark attempted to come after him. Its head popped out of the water and its mouth opened widely and went *shut*. If Joe's foot was an inch lower, it could have been chomped off painfully, aggressively, and violently.

Ian saw the crystal with joy. Joe had taken and gotten it back.

Mission success.

It was done.

When Joe got onto the sand, he crumbled and collapsed, choking out salt water and bits of weed.

"Scary, horrible, I am not doing that ever again! It will stick with me permanently!" Joe cried like he was traumatized. "You don't know how bad it was!"

"Well, at least we got the crystal back, and you are alive!" Ian replied. "Am I right?" he added. "Yes," Joe responded. "Where are the others?"

"I do not know," Ian told him. "Oh, really?" Joe retorted. "Yeah," Ian corroborated. "Let's find them," Joe answered.

They found them an arcade. Jarret was playing a pinball game while Drake was driving a motorcycle. Reeve was playing on a crane machine and Alexis was in a picture booth. "Let's go," Joe cried. "That is enough, we are leaving!" Joe announced.

"What? Come on! Why can't we stay a bit longer?" Reeve asked, rotating the crane and pressing the button. The crane dropped and clenched a sliver bear. But when it went back up, the bear fell out of its grip.

"No! I hate you!" Reeve screamed. Random strangers turned to look at her with disgust read on their faces.

"Oh, sorry," Reeve returned.

With much effort, Joe got them out of the arcade as they groaned over and over again, which was pretty annoying to Ian.

"Oh, back to the wilderness ahead!" Jarret pointed out. "I will miss Paya," he added with a hint of sadness.

And together, they went into the woods and beyond.

"Once again," Ian said.

Chapter Fifteen: Shadows and Tricks

After trudging through yet another tree land, they found themselves facing miles of dead trees that had stubborn brown leaves still clinging on the branches.

"Um, I don't think we should go into there, it looks kind of creepy," Drake raised his hand, shoving it in front of Joe.

"I know, I know, I know!" Joe cried. It was true he was distraught for some reason. "Let me think for a moment!"

Drake turned his raised his hands downside up to say that he was just giving his own opinion and suggesting.

Ian studied the ram pikes. Something was not right about them. Thick lines of leaves were tied to each of them. They were entangled. Ian wondered why. Was it a work of nature? It wouldn't be so precise.

"I need to drink water," Drake complained. "Is there any water here?" he asked. "Stop!" Joe screamed angrily.

"Oh…" Jarret blurted. Reeve looked tired and exhausted. Alexis kept quiet and didn't speak a word.

White fog flew around the forest. "No other choice, stick together," Joe lead the way into the forest of ram pikes.

"Oh boy," Alexis said.

"My eyes hurt," Jarret said. "Deal with it," Ian told his cousin. "My nose burns," Jarret said. "Don't scare me, you know I won't be by you!" Ian answered, but somehow had a little tremor in his voice. "My mouth! My face! Help! You don't know what I am going through! I cannot continue on! Help!" Jarret fell.

Ian caught him before his head fell on a stone stuck into the dry ground. There had been a drought there. Cracks were in the ground. It was very rocky.

"Joe! I actually think we are in the wrong place!" Ian cried. "I mean, what is this white fog?" Ian started choking.

"We are moving north, right? This is the only route, no detour!" Joe responded. "I don't believe that!" Ian replied.

"Well then, you tell me what!" Joe screamed. "Dude, calm down, you have anger problems," Ian said. That made Joe infuriated. "No!"

But before Ian could continue, he saw a shadow appear and then disappear. Ian's eyes went deadlocked.

"Guys, we are in trouble, we have to hide!" Ian told the crew.

After a few more glimpses of shadows, Ian knew what caused the shadows were jumping around in the top of the ram pikes. Then it made sense. The lines of leaves were like bridges. But how could they support an organism that can cause a shadow that big?

There was a whistling sound, and an arrow hit ground and stayed there, suspended, its head in the dirt.

All around them, elves jumped off the top of the ram pikes and surrounded them. They weren't green, but gray.

They went to the side to make a path for their leader. "Hello, shall I present myself?" His eyes darted around each of them. "I figure it would be best because of courtesy, so, I am the DEK, abbreviated for Dark Elf King. No one should try to mess with me," he said.

"Oh, you…" Reeve stepped forward. "Ah! My old friend!" DEK said. "No, enemies," Reeve corrected.

"Oh, how sad. I supposed we could become allies despite our differences. For example, our races, am I heard?" DEK spoke.

"You tracked us down?" Reeve questioned. "Oh! I think you can decide upon that!" DEK replied with a serious smile. "I remember you were a very intelligent person," he said.

"Run," Reeve whispered to Ian. "They will kill us all!" she added.

"They are not corrupted. They will not take money in exchange for life. They are the most loyal to The Haunter. They are not negotiable. We better leave and go!"

Ian nodded. The rest of the team got the message and sprinted, charging through several of them to break free.

"Quickly! Faster! They will chase after us!" Reeve beckoned.

"If you don't want to lose your life or die, then drive yourself!" she cried. "Let's go! They will make sure we are dead!" And they went, away from the evil Dark Elves.

Ian wanted to stop and catch his breath, but not for the sake of his life.

Chapter Sixteen: Burn the Food!

The Dark Elves were unrelenting. They caught up easily maybe because they were trained for running especially. "Hey! We are nearing the Dock Zone! We have to board a random ship that will take us across to the next continent!" Joe cried breathlessly. The lactic acid was jolting up. Ian knew it because of a lack of enough oxygen. He used to be on track in his middle school, but what either second-to-last or dead-last place. They were not going to get there.

And before Ian knew it, the Dark Elves were only feet behind him. Oh, please, Ian thought. I need to live!

A gray hand clasped his shoulder, bringing him down. He heard his friends cry something at him, but couldn't hear the phrases. What would happen next?

Ian's vision came back and he was on the ground, impotent. A spear-head came down, towards his chest. The tip was sharper than anything human-made.

The spear somehow flew away as Ian closed his eyes, waiting for impact. Ian felt thuds and people falling. There was also a blue flash of light and metal.

160

"Flix! Flix! Is that you?" Ian groaned. "Yup, you are certainly correct!" Flix replied, extending a hand out. Ian took it and he pulled him up. Ian balanced himself.

"What did you do?" Ian asked. "Oh! I killed them with this saw and disposed their bodies behind some grass…"

"What about the DEK?" Ian asked. "Uh what? Ok! No…not that guy, he wasn't here, I think he left and sent his minions at you instead," Flix replied.

"Oh well," Joe broke in, "Let's go!" Joe wasn't surprised to see Flix. In fact, he wasn't very enthusiastic.

They dragged themselves for another half an hour before approaching the Dock Zone. Boats, both private and for business were docked there. It was pretty much a strand of shoreline where ships and boats were docked.

"Hey, we need to sneak ourselves into one of those ships before they depart!" Joe told the group. "Why?" Flix asked. "Duh! We are broke!" Joe retorted. "Haven't you considered me?" "What about you is so important?" "I have the cash, paper money in my possession right now, so don't worry about going through all that!"

"Do you have enough for us all?" Joe challenged him. "Of course! I always have enough, do you doubt me?" Flix said.

"Can we just eat some dinner before boarding?" Jarret asked. "Um, yeah! We have enough time..." Flix replied.

They went to a restaurant named Crabs and Lobster's Insanity! Ian thought it was a terrible name for an eatery.

On the menu, every single plate had seafood including beverages. "Too much cholesterol!" Alexis pointed out. "Does it seriously matter?" Drake asked her.

Ian took a bite of his cheddar biscuit with shrimp in between. He had forgotten how food tasted like. His tummy roared with laughter at the sound of food.

After the meal, it was the best Ian felt in days or even a week.

They boarded the ship and it departed. Ian, in his personal room had to share with Jarret. He stepped into the shower. Ian had not bathed in almost a month. The water seemed to turn brown as it went down the drain. Ian didn't know how long he was in there. Ian fell asleep afterwards in a white bed. Hours passed.

Knock, knock, and knock! Jarret opened the door to see Joe standing there. "Yes? How may I help...?" Joe pushed Jarret aside and woke Ian up suddenly.

"We are here...time to go," Joe announced. "Just a few more minutes," Ian grumbled, his eyes closing. "Up!" Joe took the white bed sheets and flung them into the air. "By the way, your friends are watching you!"

Ian's hair was uncombed, and he was still in his pajamas.

"Out! I will get up, just...out!" Joe marched out of the room along with Jarret and shut the door, leaving Ian alone.

"Evil!" Ian spat to the ground. "Argh! Why? Why send such bad fortune on me?" Ian was extremely flustered. "I haven't had a good night sleep in, I don't know, I have lost count...I think a long time!" he said to himself.

Ian hastily got dressed and brushed his teeth because they stunk.

Ian was so cranky that he threw his pants across the room when he couldn't get his legs through the openings.

Finally, he exited his room with a card that acted like a key.

Ian nearly punched the wall when he saw that he friends had not waited for him the entire time but restrained.

He saw a little note on the carpet-floor that told him to meet them in the lobby, and if he took too long, they would just get off the ship and leave without him.

Ian went into the elevator, and its doors closed. The elevator slowly lowered downwards. Then it stopped.

Ian waited, a tad impatiently, for the doors to slid open. They never did. Then Ian started to feel apprehensive. This cannot be, he thought. Ian tried to pry open the doors, but had no luck in doing so.

He kept pressing the button that read 'ground level' slowly in the beginning but then quicker. After trying almost 100 times, Ian worked on the button that had a picture of a fireman's hat. Even worse, the lights went off.

Ian breathed big gulps of air for several seconds before the elevator's lights came back on. Ian release a sigh of relief.

People say if there is an advantage, there is also a disadvantage always. Ian didn't really believe that, but boy was he wrong. The elevator *dropped*. It dropped like it was falling down in midair.

Ian screamed. He was impotent. He would starve to death or just die right now. The plunging suddenly ended.

Yes, Ian thought. It's over. He almost forgot his Wrist Striker was still strapped to the lower half of his arm permanently according to feel. It felt like part of him.

"I'm blasting my way out, baby!" Ian exclaimed, shooting a hole out of the metal. Ian stepped out and almost fell to his death. He was still 30-35 feet in the air. Ian was completely agoraphobic.

Cable wires held the elevator in place. Ian wasn't sure if touching them were okay at all. And then, a deluge of light appeared. Ian looked up and saw the faces of his teammates, or maybe not. They were grinning a lot.

What is this? A prank? Ian thought. He felt much betrayed.

Ian climbed up and went into the compartment.

165

"Not funny at all, guys. Too serious of a prank. Too much, over the limit. I was scared to death! You guys have scared me for life…who thought of it?" Ian demanded.

They all pointed at Joe.

"Why didn't you just stop him?" Ian questioned. "Well, me, Jarret, and Reeve agreed with this plan and idea, but not Alexis. At the end, majority wins, plus she gave in and we convinced her easily!" Drake retorted.

"Joe! I'm very so much disappointed in you. You have let me down, old man! I thought we were close buds, but not anymore. This was totally absurd and ridiculous!" Ian announced.

Ian turned away and headed to the stairwell down to the lobby.

He was not in a good mood.

Ian felt like Joe had let him down. But even more anger came from the fact that Alexis was convinced easily, according to Drake. Ian wanted to just fall sleep and wake up the next day so he would not have to go through this awkwardness.

"Come on! This was just a way to teach you a lesson to hurry up with the team!" Joe slapped the back of Ian's head.

"Do not, touch me, or I will…" Ian started. "Can't you find any humor in this?" Joe asked innocently. "No! Not at all!" Ian shouted. "Oh, Ian has some anger issues," Reeve muttered to Drake. "What was that?" Ian asked. "Tell me or…!" "Whoa man, just calm down," Jarret commented. "How can I? What if it happened to you? I thought you were my cousin, who should be on my side!" Ian yelled.

The anger went away at noon. Joe took them to a fast-food restaurant. Flix had gone for the night and came back to pay the bill. Ian ate his cheese burger and immediately felt better. Joe said they needed to go south to get home. They had arrived in Toop, which was a city coated, or covered with ice, literally.

"I cannot believe this whole quest was for nothing!" Joe said. "I mean, the Shadow Clan did not even accept our gift!" Everybody went silent. "Yeah," Jarret replied only.

"It was a total waste! We put our lives in so much risk!" Joe cried. "Oh, now you are talking about it after so long?" Ian criticized. "Well, now I have the time to think about this, not before," Joe retorted.

"Save your saliva, keep moving and have that mouth shut!" Ian said.

So they went through the middle of nowhere, switching and alternating between terrains of grass and trees.

"It's all too familiar," Alexis commented. "We are getting close, I know it, to home after a prolonged *walk*!"

After what seemed like forever going nature, grain started appearing along with barns built in the center of those farms.

Cows, sheep, goats, pigs, and many more livestock became present.

"Yes, it is starting to look like home!" Drake announced.

Then, cotton fields started appearing, so as corn ones. "The farmlands. This place is where fresh produce is grown and shipped to everywhere in the world. Just this one area is our main food source," Alexis pointed out. "Learned it in social studies, ha!" she added.

Reeve seemed like she was not used to the farmlands. "I don't get it, why do people domesticate animals? It is so weird!" Reeve asked. Ian figured she would find out.

"This does not look like the tropics, or even close to it! Not at all!" Reeve wondered. "Yeah, you will adjust," Ian said back.

Maple trees, oak trees, and a lake stood in front of them. "See? Not too bad, right? Gorgeous!" Ian presented. Reeve did not look like she cared.

The farms surrounded them, but did not stop appearing. It was a very important piece of land that was fertile enough to grow crops and had an abundant supply of food for animals. This place was where the entire world depended on and much relied on.

"Yo! Let's settle and rest for a while…" Drake suggested. Joe looked like he wanted to keep going but gave in because he indeed was exhausted too.

The sky, by now, was clogged up with clouds, emitting little sunlight. It was pretty dark already.

They sat in a wheat field, huddling together. "It is so cold!" Reeve complained. "I hate this weather! It's hideous!" Reeve always used the h-word for some reason. It was a very strong one she should never use, but who can stop one arrogant and adamant girl?

Flix reappeared by Ian. "Something smells very fishy here, literally," Flix told them. Alexis scrambled up and looked around. "Uh, no, nothing!" Alexis confirmed.

Flix took his hand and swiped a finger across the tip of a strand of wheat. A black inky liquid shone on his finger. "That is an unknown fluid! Why touch it?" Reeve asked him. "It is not harmful to me, do not worry, I will be fine..." Flix trailed off.

"Poison, deadly poison, enough to kill with just one drop on skin or tongue...get out of the fields!" Flix cried.

Joe was the first to run out, followed by Alexis. Ian was a tad confused as everyone ran away.

"Get out! Now!" Flix literally screamed at him. Ian answered, "Oh!" and went out of the wheat fields.

Flix materialized next to them and said, "Whoever it is, they are trying to poison the whole world and get away with it. This will start a new world wide epidemic! We have to get rid of these crops!"

"Is it just the wheat or...?" Drake asked.

"No! Every single crop in this area is contaminated and has already assimilated the poison into their roots!" Flix shouted. "Here, take these sticks…and," he took out a lighter, "Hold them steady," lighting each, one by one, "All right, now we have to burn all these crops before they get to anyone in the world!"

Ian ran with Reeve and Alexis to the left, through a barn. "Remember! Just one touch of fire, and it will start a domino effect!" Flix yelled after them.

The barn smelled like any ordinary barn would. It was so bad Ian had to cover his nose. The animals inside made sounds as they passed by them. The horses' *hee-hawed* while the cows *mooed*.

He exited the barn and gave the carrots a touch of the torch. They caught fire, and before you know it, the entire row was burning. Steam rose to the sky.

"Burn the food! We have to stop this before it starts! It is better to have no food source than to have one that can potentially kill them. This is for the sake of our people!" Flix yelled into the dark atmosphere.

A wildfire had broken out.

"We need to escape!" Joe waved his hand. "Over here!"

"I've got it! Leave it to me!" Ian jogged over because he was out of breath. "Ok," he blurted breathlessly.

"Everybody together?" Ian spawned a bubble that trapped his friends including himself. The fire came within feet of them. "Ah! Hurry!" Ian exclaimed. The bubble seemed like it was taking its time. "No, no, no!" Ian punched the roof of it. It accelerated and shot up into the sky as the flames engulfed where they were a second before. "We did it!" Ian cried with happiness. His friends were stunned.

"How in the world did you do that?" Alexis asked. "Skills, intelligence, and experience!" Ian retorted.

"You saved us, I have got to say thank you!" Drake shook Ian's hand like a formal man. Ian just nodded in response.

"Guys, I did not know about this, it was just a reaction to my madness!" Ian told them. "Well, whatever it was, it saved us!" Drake praised the hidden power.

"Wow, what a surprise!" Ian replied.

Chapter Seventeen: Joe's Last Stand

The bubble landed on a terrain of dried dirt. Flix could not ride it because he was made of metal and was too heavy.

"We are half-a-mile from Tache! Who wants to go get some equipment for further use if we need? Let's vote!" Joe said.

"No, we can't. They do not allow outsiders to enter the city. You have to have a certain amount of money to be qualified and eligible. You see, it is a rich city, and all the money actually go to them. Tache is like a city where there are no jobs and the wealthy can relax all they want and still receive money from people like us," Alexis pointed out.

"That is pretty unfair! They control the economy of the world? What?" Reeve looked at her. "Yup, this is the truth. The fact is indeed a fact!" Alexis retorted.

"So we can't stop there, I got it," Joe responded. "Why?" "I just thought we could have some more rest time..." Joe answered. "Oh, I thought we were trying to get home instead of fooling around for some time and having fun beforehand," Alexis replied.

"I am trying to do both," Joe said.

"So, Joe, where are we heading next? I mean to?" Ian asked him. "Let me see..." Joe pulled out a travel-sized map of Adolko and pointed to where they were. "We are going to Mount Orso!" "Another mountain?" Alexis came over. "No other way, girl, or we can take the longer route, through the artic bay of massive ice craters, I said it wrong all right," Joe answered. "But what about getting on another ship so we can avoid this line of mountains?" Alexis asked. "There are no more ships in this region," Joe replied.

"Okay, I understand, I see," Alexis said. "You really do?" Joe asked for confirmation. "Yeah," she answered him.

For the next hours, Ian had a good chat with Joe and they told stories to each other. They kept breaking into laughter. Drake and Jarret would try to join the conversation a few times, but fail in doing so.

Mount Orso was even higher than The Mountain of Day and Night, where Ian and his friends had once encountered dragons hidden in them. The summit and peak was hidden behind clouds from the underside.

"How are we going to climb that thing up and over?" Jarret thought.

"If I can do it, young boy, then you can surely do it too!" Joe patted Jarret's back. "You think so?" Joe added. "Yes, but one objection. You cannot do it, I can tell!" Jarret retorted. "Oh, wait till you watch me! I will get up there in no time!" Joe replied and winked.

A sign engraved on a tree trunk read, "Welcome to Mount Orso National Park for hiking, skiing, tours, and much more. Park opens at 9:00am and closes at 5:00pm. Welcome center up ahead to the left. Thank you for reading! Have a fabulous time! We hope you enjoy!" "Very colloquial!" Alexis commented about the writing. "Of course! It is supposed to be!" Reeve told Alexis.

From the visitor center to the base of the mountain where the first trails appeared, there was a thick line where no trees were planted on, leaving it open.

"Let's go!" Joe cried.

They went within 15 feet of Mount Orso and then suddenly, the leaves on the trees started vibrating and shaking.

What was going on?

A helicopter appeared with six men, faces covered up.

A small opening was for their eyes. They carried assault rifles. They backed-away and The Breaker strode up to Joe.

"I have reason to arrest you all here because my majesty has marked you people a threat to his notorious plan..." The Breaker announced. How did he track them down?

"Well, I am so sorry we cannot come with you, because we really need to get home!" Joe said with a confident body gesture that seemed like it. It might have been or not. But what was it really deep down inside and in the interior discarding the exterior?

"Ok then, we will have to force your living souls onto this copter! Bring them up!" The Breaker spoke.

Two of the covered-up men took Joe's wrists and brought him aboard. One grabbed the back of Ian's shirt.

The helicopter rose into the air and went up, up, and up. The pressure intensified as it gained altitude.

"Welcome aboard! I present you my crew from Dop, also known as the permanent rebellious city! They are terrorists!" The Breaker introduced with a grin.

Then everything went white. The clouds. The helicopter shot out of them and landed on a clearing.

"Everybody out, out, and out!" The Breaker demanded and ordered.

"It is time for the executions to occur!" The Breaker announced. Ian was horrified. They had been caught and now were about to be slaughtered. It was too much.

"No! Please. You and me, wrestle match, one on one. Winner takes all that sound good?" Joe put his hands up. "No way, you are too weak to wrestle with me! Nobody has ever won me! I am the strongest man in the universe! A very daring idea, but not worth it at all to attempt! I mean, you actually think you can beat me?" The Breaker asked. "I am serious, I am taking on the challenge that will probably cost my life! I think I can beat you myself without any help!" Joe concluded. "Ok, then. As you wish. Bring it on, human!" The Breaker cried.

Joe ripped his T-shirt off in a swoop of his hand. He had become more muscular than before. Maybe it was because of all those push-ups and workouts he did.

177

"No Joe! Don't do it, you will lose! Are you out of your mind?" Alexis shouted. "I am the chaperone, and forever will be," Joe spoke back, not even turning his head. "I protect whoever I need to protect!"

And with that, Joe charged and wrapped his arms around The Breaker's legs, flinging him over onto his side.

"What the…" The Breaker started. He got up and threw a punch. Joe dodged his head only and put The Breaker into a headlock. The Breaker broke free and elbowed Joe's chest squarely. Joe fell on his back.

The Breaker took a piece of stone from the ground and threw it directly at Joe's forehead and missed. Joe army-crawled away. The Breaker threw another one, it hit the back of Joe's head. Another one hit his ear and side where the temple was. Joe collapsed.

Alexis was screaming on the side while Ian just stood there speechless. The terrorists still held Ian and his friends in place.

Joe stood back up and he and The Breaker grabbed each other. They pushed and applied force on each other. The terrorists decided to join in and help with the struggle.

Joe took out the terrorists easily with his feet by kicking them off the summit and letting them fall to their deaths.

When Joe was not looking, The Breaker took him and slammed him on the rocks. It was painful to watch Joe squinting in agony. Joe began to lose his energy.

Joe had one last trick in stall. He put out his leg and The Breaker tripped on it. He wobbled right on spot for a few seconds before his body went backwards and fell off the summit. Ian could not believe it. Joe had won.

Ian and his friends were so excited that they went to Joe's side to praise him. But they found him severely wounded from head to toe. He was losing a large amount of blood that was spilling out. He could not move.

"Ian! Ian!" Joe's voice was fading. His mouth was twitching. "I have something to tell you!" Ian kneeled before him. Joe was laying on a rock, his head resting on top of it as if it was a pillow.

"Joe! You are going to make it, you will go to the hospital and come out fine!" Ian said, finding hesitation in his own voice.

Drake, Jarret, Alexis, Reeve, and Flix who had just materialized gathered around them. "No, I won't. Now listen, my time is up, The Haunter is pure evil. All he wants to do is rule this world. As a chaperone, I have learned not to give into pure evilness but deal with it as a first priority. Please, don't let this happen, I know you can do it," Joe coughed. "Don't forget these words ever, it is my time to rest in peace now…" and right there Joe passed-away with his eyes open, staring at the sky. Joe was a legacy.

Ian had tears rolling down his cheeks. Alexis did too, so did Reeve, Jarret, and Drake. Flix didn't say anything but grabbed his hand and said a prayer. They watched Joe in silence. He had gone a long way from their school janitor to a hero.

Joe had gone through a lot with them and it was time for Ian to be the new chaperone even though he wasn't an adult yet. Joe's destiny had been fulfilled and Ian was going to finish it no matter how hard it was.

Ian could see that The Haunter's army was set and marching to his hometown Yart. Zartees, Sloogpaps, Dark Elves, you name it! The war had just begun.

Note to Readers:

Hey fans! Stay tuned for the finale of the Lanterncup series, book 4 is coming out soon! This novel will attract action-lovers if you are one because of the packed-action in most of the chapters. A few battles will take place in this one.

So if you are bored and have nothing to do but just read, I guarantee this will be the one for you to speed time up and enjoy the story. Your imagination is what matters most. I know that you might picture some scenes differently, but that is perfectly okay. I hope my books will inspire you to become creative and not be afraid to jot them down and publish them. When it is just down to videogames, think of a more productive thing. Not just writing, but it can be anything else. Search for your hidden talent and hobby that you have least expected.

Sincerely and Best Regards,

Marcus Tay

About the Author:

12 year old boy Marcus Tay enjoys coming home to sit on his dining chair and type whatever comes to mind. He has intense patience of writing. He has started with an average of a page an hour to 4-5 pages an hour. Schoolwork is not an obstacle to him. Marcus makes sure both are done. "Writing feels like my second nature and passion," says Marcus. It really was due to his staying up late to finish his book. Marcus typed and typed up to 12:30am on a school day. Marcus was extremely tired the next day and suffered a headache, but he knew it was worth the consequence. He lives in Northern Virginia with his motivating and proud parents.